OXFORD WORLD'S CLASSICS

LONGUS

Daphnis and Chloe

Translated with an Introduction and Notes by
RONALD McCAIL

OXFORD
UNIVERSITY PRESS

OXFORD
UNIVERSITY PRESS

Great Clarendon Street, Oxford OX2 6DP

Oxford University Press is a department of the University of Oxford.
It furthers the University's objective of excellence in research, scholarship,
and education by publishing worldwide in

Oxford New York

Auckland Bangkok Buenos Aires Cape Town Chennai
Dar es Salaam Delhi Hong Kong Istanbul Karachi Kolkata
Kuala Lumpur Madrid Melbourne Mexico City Mumbai Nairobi
São Paulo Shanghai Singapore Taipei Tokyo Toronto

with an associated company in Berlin

Oxford is a registered trade mark of Oxford University Press
in the UK and in certain other countries

Published in the United States
by Oxford University Press Inc., New York

First published as an Oxford World's Classics paperback 2002
Reissued 2009

British Library Cataloguing in Publication Data

Data available

Library of Congress Cataloging in Publication Data
Longus.
[Daphnis and Chloe. English]
Daphnis and Chloe / Longus ; translated with an introduction and notes by Ronald McCail.
p. cm.—(Oxford world's classics)
Includes bibliographical references and index.
1. Daphnis (Greek mythology)–Fiction. I. McCail, Ronald. II. Title. III. Oxford
world's classics (Oxford University Press).
PA4229.L8 E5 2002 883′.01—dc21   2001044801

ISBN 978–0–19–955495–9

3

Typeset in Ehrhardt
by RefineCatch Limited, Bungay, Suffolk
Printed in Great Britain by
Clays Ltd, St Ives plc

CONTENTS

ACKNOWLEDGEMENTS

I am obliged to Mr Gordon Howie, who found time to discuss with me some of the more perplexing passages of the Greek, and to the advisers and editors of Oxford University Press, whose observations enabled me to improve the style and accuracy of the translation in many places. Professor Charles Jones and Dr Elias Nikolakopoulos instructed me in matters of animal husbandry, Mr Graham Hardy allowed me to consult him about the vitex shrub, and Professor Ian Whyte acquainted me with the terminology of rowing. Dr Mary Whitby gave me valuable advice when publication was first being contemplated, and I owe my cover-picture to the scholarship of Mr Roger Tarr. My patient and efficient typists were Ms Elaine Hutchison and Dr Louise Maguire. It is a pleasure to acknowledge my debt to them all, and to offer them my sincere thanks.

INTRODUCTION

The Author's Intention

Many people have heard of *Daphnis and Chloe* and know that it is a tale about a pair of lovers in a pastoral setting, but few could name its author or recount the story or say what there is about it that has made it a classic. The extraordinary potency of the theme as an inspirer of works in other media has led to a situation where the reinterpretations—Ravel's orchestral suites, for example, or the lithographs of Chagall—are better known than the original. Yet, for readers today, *Daphnis and Chloe* is one of the most accessible and easily appreciated of Greek books.

In its essence, the story is timeless and universal. Daphnis and Chloe, a youth and a girl, are of an age to begin sexual intercourse. They are strongly attracted to one another, and have ample opportunity. But they have never heard of love, and do not know how to accomplish the physical act. They need to be taught, and this teaching is given in delicately humorous passages which, though perfectly explicit, are free from any taint of lubricity. To impart this instruction was one of the author's purposes in writing the book—he says so in his Preface, and there is no reason why we should not take his words at face-value. A second purpose was to 'heal the sick and cheer the desponding'; these words, too, probably mean exactly what they say, because it is known that the Greeks gave thought to how literature might be made a cure for impotence and depression. The curative properties of *Daphnis and Chloe* are its sentimental theme, the sweetness of its narrative-tone, and the optimistic view that it takes of the relationship between man and his environment, both natural and supernatural.

There is, moreover, an aspect of *Daphnis and Chloe* which appeals particularly to modern taste. In the society that it describes, nobody is an outcast. A courtesan and a homosexual are used by Divine Providence as instruments for good, the old as well as the young play a significant part, and some of the principal characters are slaves. So the story reflects the tolerance and inclusiveness which were redeeming features of ancient life.

Longus, His Date and Place of Origin

A translator introducing readers to a work of Greek literature might naturally be expected to begin with an account of the ancient author, when he lived and where he lived. In the case of *Daphnis and Chloe*, however, these matters can only be treated in a tentative and hypothetical way. There are arguments for dating the composition of the book somewhere in the several decades before or after AD 200. But these arguments have to be based entirely on style and language, because the author sets his story at a much earlier time, the fifth or the fourth century BC, and makes no allusion to any historical event contemporary with himself, or indeed to any datable event whatsoever. The manuscripts which transmit the book give the author's name as Longus, but they tell us nothing about him.[1] Outside the manuscripts there is not a single known reference to this Longus in the whole of Greek literature. How, then, is it possible to discover anything about the author?

In fact we are not altogether without resources. The scene of the story is the large island of Lesbos, situated in the eastern Aegean sea, close to where the Turkish coast is indented by the Gulf of Edremit (ancient Adramyttium). Lesbos was famous in antiquity as the birthplace of the lyric poets Sappho and Alcaeus. The picture that Longus gives of the physical geography of Lesbos is accurate enough to suggest personal acquaintance. He describes the extensive beaches, the coastal tracts exposed to pirate-raids and consequently given over to pastoralism, the rival towns of Mytilene and Methymna, the fields and woods, and, on the hill-slopes, the vineyards where the vines were cultivated in a low-spreading fashion peculiar to the Greek islands. The fauna and the flora and the climate of Lesbos (including the possibility

---

[1] They give the name in its Greek form, Longos. (One manuscript misspells it as Logos.) I shall observe convention by using the Latin form of this name.

of snow in winter) are all as described by Longus. The canal which linked the two harbours of Mytilene is also referred to, though in altered form, Longus writing as though there were a number of waterways.

From the evidence of the text, therefore, it appears that Longus knew Lesbos at first hand or by family tradition. But we can say more than this. A Greek inscription found at Mytilene, and dating from the last century BC or the first century AD, mentions a certain Gnaeus Pompeius Longus in a list of eminent citizens of Mytilene.[2] Since our author shares the cognomen 'Longus' with this personage it is possible that he belonged to a later generation of the Pompeian family.[3] This Greek family is well known; among its ancestors was the statesman Theophanes of Mytilene, historian of Pompey the Great, whose name the family took when Theophanes received the gift of Roman citizenship from the triumvir himself. We know from another (undated) inscription that one of its members, Aulus [Pompei]us Longus Dionys[odor]us, was a chief priest at Mytilene.[4] Some of the family moved to Italy, and Pompeia Agrippinilla, a direct descendant of Theophanes of Mytilene, was the wife of a Roman who held the consulship in AD 150. She was also a priestess of Dionysus and leader of a society of initiates of the god which had its meeting-place somewhere in the vicinity of Torre Nova, in the Roman Campagna.[5] This aristocratic and pious family of Mytilene would make a suitable background for the author of *Daphnis and Chloe*. And if the Pompeian family professed a special devotion to Dionysus,[6] this might be a reason why, as we shall see, Dionysus is given prominence in our story.

---

[2] *Inscriptiones Graecae* XII 2, ed. W. R. Paton (Berlin, 1899), no. 88.

[3] As suggested by C. Cichorius, *Römische Studien* (Leipzig–Berlin, 1922), 323.

[4] *Inscriptiones Graecae* XII 2, no. 249. Pompeius Longus Gallus, one of the consuls of AD 49, may have belonged to this family. But in his case we do not know of any Mytilenean connection. See *Prosopographia Imperii Romani saec. I. II. III. Pars III*, ed. P. von Rohden and H. Dessau (Berlin, 1898), 67, no. 470.

[5] See *American Journal of Archaeology*, 2nd ser., 37 (1933), 215 ff. Agrippinilla maintained her connection with Mytilene, as did her daughter, Cethegilla: see *Inscriptiones Graecae* XII 2, nos. 236 and 237.

[6] This is indicated both by Agrippinilla's priestly office and by the name Dionys[odor]us ('Gift of Dionysus') borne by the chief priest at Mytilene, above.

Perhaps we should accept the probability that Longus was a native of Mytilene and a member of this distinguished family, while acknowledging that the chain of evidence is not complete.

Daphnis and Chloe *in the Tradition of Ancient Romance*

Although *Daphnis and Chloe* is the best-known of the Greek romances, it is far from being a typical example of the genre. Writers of romances normally followed a programme in which there were certain favourite themes. The main characters are a newly married couple or a betrothed couple or a pair of lovers. Some mishap causes them to be separated and conveyed far apart from one another: pirates or brigands usually provide the mechanism for this separation. Both travel far over land and sea, and Egypt, a land of wonder to the Greeks, is commonly among their destinations. They are sold into slavery, and their chastity is assailed by a lustful master or mistress. Their lives are repeatedly endangered, by warfare or cruel punishments. There are trial-scenes. On the divine plane there is some power which protects or harasses the mortal couple, communicating with them through dreams and oracles. At last the lovers are reunited, by the agency of chance, or with the help of well-wishers or faithful slaves.

When we compare *Daphnis and Chloe* with this pattern, we find that some of the traditional elements are completely absent, while some have been subtly altered to serve a purpose very different from the literal and circumstantial recording which characterizes the other writers. In Longus' universe, no firm boundary is set between the human and the divine, and man lives in harmony with his neighbours, who are the animals and plants and rivers, the winds and the seas. All are interpenetrated by deity, in a pantheism reminiscent of that imagined by the young William Wordsworth. This element of *Daphnis and Chloe* can fairly be called mysticism, and more will be said about it in a later section of the Introduction. Only in the countryside, amid the tranquillity of familiar scenes, can these influences be perceived. It follows that Longus' story has no need of far-flung journeyings— Daphnis and Chloe remain in the same locality throughout, with only brief interruptions. There are alarms and adventures, of course, because man has free will and sometimes does wrong. But the gods always act quickly to restore the proper order.

This is not to suggest that *Daphnis and Chloe* belongs anywhere but in the tradition of romance. Many of the standard ingredients are there, only Longus' treatment of them is idiosyncratic and influenced by his whole intention. We are given a trial-scene, but the court sits out of doors and the judge is a cowherd. There are pirates and an invasion of enemies—Daphnis is captured by the former and Chloe by the latter; but when both are delivered, it is by the power of music, and not by arms. Both Daphnis and Chloe are beaten, but the violence is haphazard and there is no torture. Daphnis is seduced by a woman of experience; but this is a necessary initiation, and no sin. This episode is treated without the prurience to be found in the *Leucippe and Cleitophon* of Achilles Tatius, and in the *Metamorphoses* of the Latin writer Apuleius and its Greek equivalent, *Lucius, or The Ass*, by Lucian of Samosata.

Plot Elements

The Picture

When launching his story, Longus employs a device which the modern reader may well find puzzling. In his Preface he tells us that *Daphnis and Chloe* is the narrative of events portrayed on a picture which he saw in Lesbos—one of the inhabitants, he says, gave him an explanation of the picture's meaning, which he now passes on to us. Longus is the narrator throughout, but we forget that he is speaking, because only once after the Preface does he say 'I', in 1.32. That the whole story is supposed to be an evocation of a picture is not something that would have caused difficulty to Longus' contemporaries; elaborate descriptions of works of art (called in Greek *ecphrases*) are found in literature from Homer onwards, and they were still in fashion when Longus wrote. A similar, though not identical, artifice is adopted by Achilles Tatius at the beginning of *Leucippe and Cleitophon*.

There, Achilles represents himself as arriving in the Phoenician city of Sidon and taking a walk to admire the buildings and monuments; his attention is caught by a picture showing Zeus in the shape of a bull, swimming to Crete with Europa on his back—Love (Eros) is leading the bull. A young stranger accosts Achilles and offers to tell him of his own sufferings at the hands of Love. He is Cleitophon, and the rest of the book is his narrative. This is a less crude procedure than making the whole story the explanation of a picture, as does Longus. Moreover, it involves a more refined narrative technique, because, while Achilles begins his story by speaking in the first person, like Longus, he continues by quoting the first-person narrative of someone else. In neither book is there mention of the initial narrator (Longus, Achilles) at the end. The silence is absolute in Achilles. In Longus, it is a little less so, since we are told in the penultimate paragraph about certain commemorative pictures set up by Daphnis and Chloe, which are surely to be identified with the picture at the beginning. Thus the reader is gently prompted to recall the Preface and Longus.

Exposure and Recognition

It was a harsh fact of ancient life that unwanted infants were often abandoned by their parents in places where there was a hope that they might be found and adopted by some childless couple. Daphnis and Chloe are exposed in this way, but in making them be suckled by a she-goat and a ewe, Longus removes the motif from real life to fantasy. They are to be regarded in the same light as the numerous figures of mythology who were reared by animals—the most familiar being Zeus (suckled by a she-goat) and the founders of Rome, Romulus and Remus (reared by a she-wolf). The tokens exposed along with Daphnis and Chloe likewise belong to fiction rather than to reality, because they were a traditional device in tragedy and comedy for bringing about the recognition of long-lost children. Recognition by means of tokens was not highly commended by Aristotle when he listed the possible modes of recognition in order of merit (*Poetics* 16). As though aware of this, Longus does not try to contrive any great degree of surprise for the scenes where Daphnis and Chloe are recognized by their parents—after all, we have known about the tokens from the start, and when an aristocratic couple are brought into association with Daphnis, it needs little acumen to guess that they will turn out to be his father and mother. Nevertheless, Longus precipitates the recognition skilfully by Gnathon's attempted rape of Daphnis. And Gnathon's misconduct leads directly to a moment of suspense, when it seems that Daphnis may kill himself before he learns of his parentage. The recognition of Chloe follows after an interval: this time, dreams and ambiguous divine intimations are involved, in addition to birth-tokens.

The Myths

Some of the most exquisite passages in the book are contained in the three myths which punctuate the narrative. These myths are not merely ornamental, but are placed significantly in their context. All three are of the type called 'aetiological'; that is, they purport to explain the reason (Gk. *aition*, cause) for something.

In 1.27 Daphnis explains to Chloe why the wood-pigeon has such a distinctive call. The boy and girl herding their cows in the myth are obviously parallel to Daphnis and Chloe, and Daphnis says that the girl resembles Chloe. Like Chloe, she wears a garland of pine-sprigs. Daphnis tells the story to enlighten Chloe's ignorance, exactly as, in Achilles Tatius (*Leucippe and Cleitophon* 5.5.1), Cleitophon enlightens Leucippe by telling her the myth of Philomela and Procne.

The second myth is told by Lamon at Daphnis' thanksgiving celebration for the rescue of Chloe from the Methymnaeans (2.34). It is the tale of Pan and Syrinx, a fanciful account of how pan-pipes were invented. This theme is relevant to the context, since Daphnis and his companions are waiting for the pipes of Philetas, the great musician, to be fetched. In the sequel, Daphnis and Chloe portray the myth in an impromptu ballet.

The third myth, at 3.23, is the story of Pan and Echo, and, like the first myth, Daphnis tells it to Chloe by way of instruction. There is a horrible climax to this tale, the tearing in pieces of the nymph Echo by shepherds whom Pan has driven mad. In its context, this dreadful event hints at the mental state of Daphnis, who, a short time before, has left Chloe's virginity intact because he is unwilling to inflict pain and bleeding on her.

Dramatic Date

Although the historical context is only lightly indicated, there is enough to show that Longus conceived his story as taking place in the fourth or the fifth century BC, when Greece was still a country of independent city-states and had not yet fallen under the domination of Macedon or Rome. Thus in *Daphnis and Chloe* the Lesbian towns of Mytilene and Methymna are free to make war or conclude peace, and their military and diplomatic procedures are those attributed by Thucydides to Greek cities in the fifth century. The pirates in 1.28 use a distinctive type of vessel, the *hemiolia*, which literary sources (Theophrastus, Arrian) confirm to have been frequently used by pirates in the fourth century. Rich men in Longus are taxed to pay for warships and dramatic productions (4.35), as they were in Athens and other cities in the fifth and fourth centuries. Daphnis and Chloe, therefore, do not live in the mythical Golden Age, but in a definable historical period. Perhaps Longus' contemporaries, made familiar with the fifth and fourth centuries by their education, would have felt a stronger sense of historical epoch in the book than readers are conscious of today.

Characters

Daphnis and Chloe

When the detailed story of their fortunes begins (1.7), Daphnis is fifteen and Chloe thirteen. We follow their life for the next year and a half, and in this time they develop from a state of complete innocence to a certain degree of experience and the beginnings of maturity. Girls grow up faster than boys as a rule, and Chloe is no exception. She is the first to fall in love, and afterwards, when the two swear oaths of fidelity, it is she who strikes a solemn note by commanding Daphnis to kill her if she is false to her oath. And when Daphnis' sexuality becomes exigent, some maidenly instinct warns her to keep her clothes on. Daphnis, too, attains discretion by the end of the story, keeping silent in the presence of his master, and prudently concealing his love for Chloe until a fitting time comes for avowal. Before this, however, he has often proved inadequate: he hides while raiders are taking Chloe prisoner, besmirches his oath by succumbing to Lycaenion, and does nothing but lament when Chloe is kidnapped by a rival. Not that he fails every test: the challenges that confront him in the pasture, whether from refractory animals or interlopers from the town, find him brave and resolute. He is a good orator, trouncing Dorcon in debate and moving the peasants deeply with his pleading against the Methymnaeans. He is, in fact, a complex figure, the more so because of his spiritual dimension. For Daphnis has been marked out for divine favour: Eros and the Nymphs and other powers are keeping a friendly eye on him, and at critical moments they pull the strings to his advantage. From them he has his knowledge of myths and his inspired musicianship. Chloe, too, is a chosen spirit. At the end, Daphnis and Chloe give lavish rewards to the gods who have protected them and united them in marriage, and we are told that their life in after-years assumes an almost priestly character.

The characteristic in Daphnis and Chloe which above all strikes modern readers is their sexual naivety. This quality of innocence may be hard to believe in, but it is a very important element in the story. Their foster-parents have sent them to school and equipped them with a trade, but they have not told them anything about Love, the god or the passion. That is because they themselves are ignorant of both. And so when Daphnis and Chloe are made by the god to fall in love, they do not know what is the matter or how it can be cured. Longus leaves us in no doubt that their ignorance is a virtue, despite its ludicrous side: at the end, Chloe's preservation of her virginity is seen to have been crucial—had she not been a virgin, Dionysophanes would not have accepted her as a daughter-in-law.

In fact, this happy outcome is not solely the result of

ignorance. For Daphnis is not ignorant after his encounter with Lycaenion—he has learned how to make love properly, and he knows what Chloe will have to endure for their love to be consummated. To spare her, he resolves to respect her virginity. With knowledge has come an adult sense of responsibility.

Lamon and Dryas, Myrtale and Nape

If Longus' picture of Daphnis and Chloe is rather fluid and impressionistic, he draws with a firmer outline when he portrays the foster-fathers, Lamon and Dryas. They are 'tough old fellows, hard-handed from their toil on the farm' (2.14), and each knows that, in his adopted child, he owns an asset that is not to be parted with cheaply. Both are slaves (though in Dryas' case this is not expressly stated); after the perennial manner of Greek agricultural slavery, they have been left in charge of the work on remote farms, and are liable to harsh penalties should they default. Lamon is the older, and he is also the cannier. This is first indicated at his discovery of Daphnis, when he thinks for a moment of taking the tokens and leaving the baby to its fate. Dryas, on the other hand, lifts up Chloe without hesitation. The contrast between the two is seen at its sharpest over the marriage negotiations, when Lamon behaves with a circumspection worthy of a diplomat. Thinking that Daphnis is too good for Chloe, he takes advantage of his own servile status to refer the decision to his master—he hopes that Daphnis will thereby be prevented from marrying Chloe. Dryas assumes that the marriage will take place; in this he is precipitate, because Daphnis' divine patrons, as well as his mortal master, have yet to give their consent, and much has still to happen. Elsewhere, Lamon displays knowledge and eloquence, recounting a myth (2.34) and speaking in poetic prose (ibid. and 4.8).[7] Dryas is an effective speaker when occasion requires, but he never tells a myth or speaks in poetic prose. He is of somewhat commoner clay than Lamon. Their wives, too, are differentiated with subtle fitness: Lamon's Myrtale (pron. Myrtalee) is the softer and more submissive, Dryas' Nape (pron. Napee) is the more managing. (*Nape*

---

[7] On poetic prose, see below, pp. xx–xxii.

means 'Glen'. But *napu*, a word close in sound, means 'mustard'!)

Gnathon

Just as Chloe has been the target of a bungled rape attempt in Book 1, so Daphnis is the object of a similar attempt in Book 4. This time the culprit is Gnathon, the parasite or dependant of the master's son, Astylus. Gnathon takes his character as a gormandizer from the gluttons of comedy (see p. xviii), but he adds to this a voracious carnal appetite for both sexes. When he makes his assault on Daphnis, he is fuddled with drink, and is easily pushed away. This is fortunate because, when sober, Gnathon is formidable. He is a convincing actor and a skilled rhetorician, and he uses these accomplishments to secure Astylus' help in a new plan to ensnare Daphnis. Gnathon also has a capacity for swift and violent action. Once, the action is discreditable, when he raises his hand to strike Lamon (a slave could not hit back). But he redeems himself by his quick rescue of Chloe from abduction, at a time when Daphnis is paralysed and unable to act. From Gnathon's passion for Daphnis results, ultimately, the discovery of the true parentage of Daphnis and Chloe. Under Divine Providence, Gnathon's impudence is made to work for good.

The Influence of Literary Genres

When he created *Daphnis and Chloe*, Longus drew on a variety of literary genres besides that of romance, and an account of these must now be given.[8]

Since *Daphnis and Chloe* tells of the life of a goatherd and a shepherdess and their rustic companions, it belongs to the branch of literature called 'pastoral' (Lat. *pastor*, shepherd.) The most venerated writer in this tradition was the poet Theocritus, who flourished *c.*280 BC. Longus writes in prose, not poetry, but his work is no less of a pastoral because of this. Indeed, its title in the manuscripts is 'The Pastorals of Longus, about Daphnis and

[8] Many of the passages mentioned in this section have been discussed by R. L. Hunter, *A Study of 'Daphnis and Chloe'* (Cambridge, 1983), 59–83.

Chloe'. Some of his happiest notions are adaptations of things that he found in Theocritus. His hero's name, Daphnis, is taken from the first *Idyll* of Theocritus (see note to p. 6). The same poem has given him the cricket-cage that Chloe plaits in 1.10, and the motifs of Daphnis wasting away for love (1.18) and the cattle mourning for the dead Dorcon (1.31). And when Lamon says that the myth of Pan and Syrinx was sung to him by a Sicilian goatherd in return for a billy-goat and a set of pipes, we are to think of the goat and the wondrously carved cup which the goatherd in the first *Idyll* gives Thyrsis for singing 'The Sufferings of Daphnis' (Theocritus, *Idylls* 1.19 ff.). The remedy that Philetas recommends to Daphnis and Chloe for the passion of love is memorable in expression and admirable in its practicality (2.7); behind it, however, lies the cure for love that Theocritus proposed to his doctor-friend Nicias in the eleventh *Idyll*—not indulgence, as in Longus, but sublimation, the composing of poetry (see note to p. 28). The several evocations of the beauty of the countryside given in *Daphnis and Chloe* are full of the spirit of Theocritus, and one, the mellow passage describing Nature's summer bounty in 3.33, is probably intended to recall the harvest festival celebrated by Phrasidamus and his friends in *Idylls* 7 (see note to p. 63). These allusions to Theocritus are not to be regarded as thefts—they constitute a second level of discourse which Longus intends his readers to notice and appreciate. The same holds good for the borrowings from the other literary genres to be mentioned in this section.

The influence of comedy is scarcely less strong. Sometimes it is manifested in a general way, and not attributable to any particular play. To this category belong the figures of Lycaenion, who resembles the kind-hearted courtesans in several plays by Menander, and of the parasite and glutton Gnathon, a type familiar in the comedy after Aristophanes. (There is a parasite called Gnathon in Menander's *Colax* (The Flatterer).) In comedy, townspeople go out to the country, slaves are threatened with punishment, old men conduct marriage-negotiations, preparations are made for weddings, recognition-tokens are displayed.

All these themes appear in *Daphnis and Chloe*. Sometimes, however, the influence of a particular play has to be considered as a possibility. At the beginning of Menander's *Dyscolus* (*The Curmudgeon*) the god Pan emerges from a grotto of the Nymphs and informs the audience that the Curmudgeon has a virtuous daughter who is soon to be rewarded for her past reverence of the Nymphs. The grotto, the association of Pan with the Nymphs, and their care for the girl recall *Daphnis and Chloe*. Later in the same play, the Curmudgeon falls into a well and has to be pulled out, an incident paralleled by Daphnis' misfortune in 1.12. When Lycaenion excuses her absence from home by telling her common-law husband that she is going to visit an expectant mother (3.15), she is repeating a subterfuge found in Aristophanes, *Ecclesiazusae* (*Women at the Assembly*) 528 f. In *Daphnis and Chloe*, the town begins to invade the countryside with Lycaenion's appearance on the scene, and from that point onwards the atmosphere of comedy gradually predominates over that of pastoral. This is especially true of Book 4. Longus seems to have preferred the comic style of Menander (342–291 BC), with its gentle and sympathetic portrayal of human weakness, to the ferocious satire of Aristophanes. In this he shares the taste of his Graeco-Roman contemporaries, who were devoted to Menander.

Homer is, of course, the paramount influence on Greek literature, and the full significance of several passages of *Daphnis and Chloe* can only be appreciated when their Homeric background is taken into account. An identification of Daphnis with the god Dionysus is hinted at in 1.28, where Daphnis is captured by pirates as he strolls alone beside the sea. So, in one of the Hymns attributed to Homer in antiquity, pirates seized the god himself while he walked

> beside the shore of the unharvested sea,
> on a jutting headland, like to a young man
> in his first manhood . . .
> (*Homeric Hymn to Dionysus* 2–4)

At his first meeting with his master Dionysophanes, Daphnis is compared to Apollo in the days when the god herded cattle for Laomedon, king of Troy, a legend told in *Iliad* 21.441–57 (see note to p. 72). This is an important moment for Daphnis, and the epic allusion endows it with dignity and, perhaps, mystery. More earthy in intention are the adaptation of a Homeric simile to describe the peasants chasing the Methymnaean interlopers (2.17), and the ironic adumbration of Penelope behind Lycaenion when she ensnares Daphnis with her tall story (3.16)—no chaste wife she! Other Homeric allusions are mentioned in the Explanatory Notes.

Little inferior to Homer in prestige was the lyric poetess Sappho (seventh to sixth century BC). From her, Longus has derived the comparison of Daphnis' pallor to summer grass in 1.17, and the description of the solitary apple—a symbol for Chloe—in 3.34.

As befits a prose author, Longus takes much from the historians. At a verbal level, he has many echoes of Herodotus, Thucydides, and Xenophon, especially the last. To illustrate this in translation would require much space. But Greekless readers can appreciate his use of two stories from Herodotus, at 2.23 and 2.27 (see notes to pp. 36 and 38). When he describes the war between Mytilene and Methymna (3.1–3), he writes in a quasi-historical style.

So *Daphnis and Chloe* is a romance and a pastoral and—in part—a comedy. The influence upon it of rhetoric remains to be considered. Ancient authors usually gave their compositions to the world by declaiming them before an audience. A literary work presented in this way is bound to have some of the characteristics of a speech, and this is one reason why rhetoric exercised so strong an influence on literature in antiquity. A second reason is to be found in the important place that rhetoric occupied in the curriculum of higher education. Graeco-Roman authors had at their disposal a number of rhetorical styles, ranging from the plain to the ostentatious. The style chosen by Longus is the one called the 'sweet' style. Some of its characteristics, as they were listed by the rhetorician Hermogenes in the later second century AD, are observable in Longus: sweet

diction,[9] figures of speech, erotic subject-matter, descriptions of
landscape, myths, quotations from poetry woven into the prose
narrative, the attribution of human intentions to animals and
inanimate things.[10] In the balance and symmetry of his expressions, Longus goes further than most writers: he makes free use
of the rhetorical figure called 'parisosis' (exact or approximate
equality in the number of syllables in parallel clauses or phrases),
sometimes supplementing it with rhyme or assonance. Hermogenes, in fact, mentions parisosis as a possible component of the
'sweet' style.[11] This element in *Daphnis and Chloe* is striking
enough for an example to be quoted. Here is the first sentence of
the Preface, given in transliterated form, and accompanied by a
literal translation:

En Lesbō thērōn	Hunting in Lesbos
en alsei Nymphōn	in a grove of the Nymphs
thëāma eidon	I saw a sight
kālliston hōn eidon,	the fairest of those that I saw,
eikonos graphēn,	a painting of a picture,
historian erōtos.	a story of love.

In the Greek, the successive phrases are of 5, 5, 5, 6, 5, and 7
syllables; the first two phrases are similar in structure, and there
is rhyme between the last syllables of *thērōn* and *Nymphōn*. The
use of parisosis continues to the end of the Preface, and there are
several other examples of end-rhyme. Once the narrative is
reached, at the beginning of Book 1, a more sober style predominates. But Longus returns to the balanced style in passages
of higher emotion throughout. These passages might be termed
'poetic prose'. I have tried to exhibit their special character by
printing them with the lineation of poetry, using marginal
indentation to show which phrases and clauses are in symmetry
with one another (see, in addition to the Preface, 1.14 and 18; 2.7
and 34; 3.34; 4.8). Some other passages could be treated in this

---

[9] But not *poetic* diction: Longus uses the standard vocabulary of contemporary literary prose.

[10] *Hermogenis Opera*, ed. H. Rabe (Teubner, Leipzig, 1913), 330–9, 344–5. See the translation and analysis of these passages given by Hunter, *A Study*, 92 ff.

[11] *Hermogenis Opera*, 344.

way, e.g. 3.23. The same features can be seen in some authors of the late second and early third centuries AD, and this gives a reason for dating Longus in this period. In its origin, however, the style was much older. It was taught by Gorgias of Leontini, a contemporary of Socrates, and developed by orators practising in the cities of Asia Minor during the last three centuries before Christ—whence it was called the 'Asian' style. Its exponents declaimed melodiously in a kind of song-speech, and it is possible that Longus delivered his most elevated passages in this way.

The Meaning of Daphnis and Chloe: *The Mystery of Eros*

Longus was as much a man of his time in his attitude to religion as in his approach to literary form. The religious aspect of *Daphnis and Chloe* was not examined until comparatively recently; but study of it provides the key to a proper understanding of the book.

In the cosmopolitan society of the Roman Empire, the traditional and official religious cults were accorded less general veneration than they had received at an earlier period. Intended as they were to lend divine sanction to the institutions of the state, they afforded only meagre nourishment to the deeper yearnings of the human spirit; and they possessed little appeal for the non-Italians who made up most of the population. At all levels of society they tended to be supplemented or replaced by other systems of belief. The educated betook themselves to philosophy, but this road was open only to a few. To the remainder, religion was still congenial, but their preference was for a religion that offered personal salvation, by giving membership of an elect of sanctified souls and holding out a promise of immortality. In the older Greek world, these aspirations had been catered for by the yearly ceremonies in honour of Demeter at Eleusis, which linked human life to the annual regeneration of Nature, and by orgiastic worship like that of Dionysus and Cybele, which claimed to give the individual communion with the god. These cults survived into the Roman Empire—the Dionysiac conventicle of Agrippinilla is an example. But they had been augmented by a multitude of religions, also promising salvation, which had entered Greece from Egypt, Persia, and the Semitic lands after the eastern campaigns of Alexander the Great. Like their older Greek counterparts, the lately arrived oriental cults reserved their innermost secrets for those who had followed a course of initiation: after performing rituals, undergoing ordeals, listening to the reading of a sacred legend, and witnessing revelations, the candidate was credited with having been reborn into a state of holiness. These initiations were called 'mysteries', from the Greek verb *myein*, 'to keep the eyes closed'. They passed from Greece to Rome, and the practice of them was rife in the Roman Empire.

It is likely, therefore, that Longus' audience at the first recitation of *Daphnis and Chloe* included initiates of one or other of the mysteries, and that, for them, certain elements of the story possessed a significance transcending their function as ingredients in the plot. Even non-initiates would have sensed the possibility of a double-meaning in phrases as suggestive as 'Daphnis and Chloe are my sheep now' (2.5), 'waited for spring, that rebirth after death' (3.4), and 'because *they* were servants of a Greater Shepherd' (3.12). And certain episodes and situations in Longus' story would surely have awakened resonances in minds habituated to the religious climate of the second or the third century AD. To be suckled by animals was, as already noted, a mark of divine or semi-divine beings. Daphnis surrounded by the sheep and goats resembles Orpheus among the animals, a frequent motif in art. Ordeals are undergone when Daphnis falls into the pit, and when he and Chloe are captured by enemies—Chloe is scourged, Daphnis buffeted. Daphnis is initiated into manhood by Lycaenion, and he in turn initiates Chloe into womanhood when they marry. There are mystical overtones in Daphnis' reunion with his father after his slavery and long exile from his inheritance (compare the parable of the Prodigal Son). The father's name, Dionysophanes, means 'Dionysus appearing'. The silence kept by Daphnis when approaching Dionysophanes suggests the silence demanded of candidates for initiation into the Dionysiac mysteries.[12] After their marriage, Daphnis and Chloe live a holy life, in which their associations and their food are all pure, and there are no evil contagions.

In the progress of Daphnis and Chloe from ignorance to enlightenment, the unifying and guiding agent is Eros/Love.[13] Longus embodies him as the mischievous boy of Graeco-Roman art and literature, but gives him at the same time attributes derived from an earlier and more awe-inspiring conception of the god. According to Hesiod, a contemporary or perhaps predecessor of Homer, Eros was born at the same time as Earth and Tartarus, and preceded only by Chaos (*Theogony* 116 ff.). This is the reason why Longus represents Eros as being older than Cronos and all Time itself (2.5). In Longus, Eros appears not to Daphnis and Chloe but to Philetas the cowherd, who describes the god to them and proclaims his powers. The two speeches of Philetas include elements familiar from Plato's *Symposium* and *Phaedrus* and from the archaic poet Alcman: thus Eros rules the gods, he makes souls grow wings, he passes his time among flowers.[14] Longus is not unique among writers of his period and later in representing Eros as the dominant power of the universe. The god's universal sway and his immemorial age occur as topics in the prose hymn to Dionysus by his contemporary Aelius Aristides, and in a set of instructions for the writing of panegyrics on the institution of marriage, compiled by the rhetorician Menander in the fourth century AD. But these lack the poetic and religious feeling of Philetas' speeches.

It is Eros who provides Longus with the material of his narrative: see 2.27, 'a girl whom Love means to make into a myth'—*Daphnis and Chloe* is that myth. The youth and girl have been consecrated to Eros (2.6), and his is the mystery into which they have to be initiated. But in Longus' mystery of Eros there is more than the sexual union of two adolescents. Fulfilling his universal, cosmic role, Eros is present in the beauty and fruitfulness of all

---

[12] See *American Journal of Archaeology* (cited n. 5 above), 262–3.

[13] In my translation I have rendered the divine name Eros as 'Love', using a capital letter to personify the English noun. In Greek, *erōs* is alike the passion and the god.

[14] See Plato *Symposium* 195c and *Phaedrus* 249d; Alcman fr. 58 Page.

Nature, animate and inanimate. When Longus describes the ripe apples falling to the earth, the corn standing high on the plains, Daphnis stripping naked to bathe, and the other concomitants of high summer, he is describing Eros, of whose presence and power all are equally manifestations. The streams in Philetas' garden, too, partake of Eros, because the god bathes in them daily; and so do the birds overhead, because all birds are descended, as Aristophanes says, from the union of Eros and Chaos (*Birds* 698). Longus is propounding a kind of pantheism of which his most explicit statement is the hymnic passage, 2.7:

> . . . All flowers are the works of Love,
> all trees are his creations;
> through his power
> do rivers flow
> and winds blow . . .

At a less exalted level, the story's value as a practical therapy (advertised near the end of the author's Preface) comes from Eros.

Eros was often linked with Dionysus in Greek tradition, and so he is in *Daphnis and Chloe*. As Eros rules spring and summer, so Dionysus rules autumn, season of the vintage. In our story, violent things happen in the autumn: the pirate-raid and the Methymnaean war, the violation of the paradise-garden, the attempted rape of Daphnis, the abduction of Chloe, and, at the very end, Chloe's deflowering by Daphnis. There is significance in the concentration of these events into the season of Dionysus. The Greeks knew that the mythology of Dionysus and the actual practice of his cult often involved violence, a state of affairs portrayed with terrifying vividness in the *Bacchae* of Euripides. This fact is acknowledged in our story, where the wall-paintings inside the temple of Dionysus (4.3) all contain violence, explicit or implied.

In the first three books of *Daphnis and Chloe*, Dionysus is present by allusion and by the manifestation of his power: Chloe wears a Bacchic fawn-skin, the vintage is described, ivy (a Dionysiac plant) appears miraculously on the horns of Daphnis' goats, Daphnis and Chloe kiss in an ivy-bower, Dryas celebrates the

festival of the Winter Dionysia. Book 4 has a second vintage-
season, and an altar and temple of Dionysus. In this book, the
name of Daphnis' real father, Dionysophanes ('Dionysus
appearing'), has been taken to imply that Dionysophanes is an
incarnation of the god, especially since he arrives just at the time
when the grape-juice has begun to ferment and become wine. But
perhaps too much ought not to be made of this: several historical
people (one of them, probably, on Lesbos) were called Dionysophanes, and the name consequently does not have to imply the
actual presence of the god. At all events, the prominence given to
Dionysus in the story is appropriate, because he was worshipped
on Lesbos from early times,[15] and we have seen reason to think
that the family of Longus may have been priests of his cult.[16]

Whereas Eros and Dionysus are universal forces, the power
exercised by Pan and the Nymphs is local and more personal.
Country people prayed to 'dear Pan' for the fertility of their fields
and animals, and they feared his mysterious emanations ('panic')
which could rout armies, as they do in *Daphnis and Chloe*. His
statue, horned and goat-legged, was a familiar sight in the Greek
countryside. So were the groves and caves and wells of the
Nymphs, hung with offerings. The Nymphs act under the providence of Eros to bring about Chloe's marriage to Daphnis. This is
partly because Chloe was entrusted to their care as an infant; but
the piety of Daphnis and Chloe, also, has won them the Nymphs'
love.

All these gods were powers of fertility, and it accords with this
that Longus places strong emphasis on the cycle of the seasons—
fertilization in spring, growth and fruition in summer and
autumn, dormancy in winter. Some of his most striking passages
are descriptions of seasonal scenes and activities. In one of these,
the description of summer in 1.23–7, another divine power is
revealed. The sun's heat causes all nature to wax and bear fruit,
and it likewise fosters desire in Daphnis and Chloe. Here, the
functions of Helios (the sun-god) and Eros blend in a way that
would have been readily intelligible to Longus' contemporaries.

---

[15] See *American Journal of Archaeology* (cited n. 5 above), 232.
[16] See above, p. ix.

From the second century AD onwards there was a strong tendency for the many gods to be looked on as different manifestations of a single divine power, called the 'Highest God' (Lat. *Summus Deus*, Gk. *Theos Hypsistos*). Eros and Helios, Eros and Dionysus, Pan and the Nymphs are pairs whose spheres of influence overlap. It may be that a monotheism underlies Longus' portrayal of divine activity, and that this, too, is a part of his mystery.[17]

From Antiquity to Modern Times

There is no sign that *Daphnis and Chloe* was read in later antiquity: we have nothing in literature that can be proved to be an allusion to it, and no representation of it on wall-painting or mosaic. This silence seems to imply that Longus' book remained where it was composed. Its hiding-place might have been the temple of Dionysus at Mytilene,[18] or it might have been preserved in a house belonging to Longus' descendants.

In Byzantium, *Daphnis and Chloe* appears twice probably and once for certain. Constantine of Rhodes (who flourished in the later ninth century), in a poem in the anacreontic metre, imagines himself chancing on Eros as the god dances with nymphs in a stream, and pursuing him through flowers and thickets; this resembles Philetas' pursuit of Eros in Longus.[19] Next, the name Bryaxes borne by a king in the twelfth-century verse-romance *Rhodanthe and Dosicles*, by Theodorus Prodromus, is very like the name of the Methymnaean general Bryaxis in *Daphnis and Chloe*. These identifications have to be made with caution, for Constantine might have been imitating some other lost model, and the name Bryaxis, though very rare, is not exclusive to

[17] My account of the mystical elements in *Daphnis and Chloe* owes much to the sensitive and profound study by H. H. O. Chalk, 'Eros and the Lesbian Pastorals of Longus', *Journal of Hellenic Studies*, 80 (1960), 32–51. This theme is also explored, with a wealth of inscriptional and pictorial illustration, in R. Merkelbach's book *Die Hirten des Dionysos* (1988).

[18] K. Tümpel suggested that *Daphnis and Chloe* was the sacred legend of this temple. See *Philologus*, 48 (1889), 115, n. 31. This is not very different from the view taken by Merkelbach, *Die Hirten*.

[19] See R. C. McCail in *Byzantion*, 58 (1988), 112–22.

Longus. But there is no doubt about the third testimony: another poet of the twelfth century, Nicetas Eugenianus, names Daphnis and Chloe, and gives a brief résumé of their history in his verse-romance *Drosilla and Charicles*.[20]

After the fall of Byzantium and the revival of learning in the West, the first translation of *Daphnis and Chloe* to appear was the French one by Jacques Amyot (1559). This is the best-known and most influential version. Other noteworthy translations of early date were those of Annibale Caro (Italian, completed by 1538 but not published until 1786), Laurenzio Gambara (1574, in Latin hexameters), and George Thornley (English, 1657).[21] The numerous translations which have been published in recent years are listed in J. R. Morgan's bibliography of Longus.[22]

From the first, *Daphnis and Chloe* appealed to readers because of the charm of its conception, the beauty of its descriptions, and its delicate humour. But the fact that it contains nudity and an act of sexual intercourse caused it to be regarded as a recherché piece of erotica—unjustly, because Longus' tact and good feeling protects him from the charge of prurience. This misjudgement influenced the attitude of classical scholars to *Daphnis and Chloe* through the nineteenth and earlier twentieth centuries, when depreciatory estimates of it were often expressed,[23] and no substantial commentary was produced. The turn of the tide was marked by G. Valley's study of the linguistic usage of Longus,[24] which prepared the way for the large amount of work done on Longus in the later twentieth century. These more recent contributions have revealed *Daphnis and Chloe* as a work of serious intention and refined literary culture.

Daphnis and Chloe cries out for illustration: and the qualities in it which repelled austere savants are precisely the ones which

---

[20] *Drosilla and Charicles* 6.439–450 (*Erotici Scriptores Graeci*, t. 2., ed. R. Hercher, Teubner, Leipzig, 1859). He also (ibid. 356–77) paraphrases portions of Longus' Preface, Daphnis' monologue (1.18), and Philetas' proclamation of Eros (2.7).

[21] For a survey of some early translations, see Giles Barber, '*Daphnis and Chloe*': *The Markets and Metamorphoses of an Unknown Bestseller* (The Panizzi Lectures, 1988: London, 1989), 1–52.

[22] See below, p. xxxvi.

[23] See the selection in Chalk, 'Eros and the Lesbian Pastorals', 32, n. 4.

[24] 'Über den Sprachgebrauch des Longus' (diss., Uppsala, 1926).

have attracted artists. The best pictorial representations emphasize the innocence and vulnerability of the two adolescents; others, however, exploit the story's carnal side. Examples of both sorts are to be found among the fourteen illustrations by various hands collected by Tomas Hägg in *The Novel in Antiquity*.[25] A delightful set of lithographs was made by Marc Chagall for an edition of the Amyot translation (1961): these have the same cheerful and uplifting quality as the story, and a physical exuberance that disarms criticism. An earlier work, however, has the highest claim to consideration. It has recently been argued that the painting by Titian traditionally called *The Three Ages of Man* (1516) was inspired by the story of Daphnis and Chloe.[26] Three passages of this painting appear to represent Eros with Daphnis and Chloe as infants, Daphnis and Chloe after the bath of Daphnis (1.13), and Dionysophanes with the skulls of his elder son and his daughter (4.24).[27] If this hypothesis is correct, the earliest illustration of *Daphnis and Chloe* is also the finest.

Over music, too, the story has exercised its power, inspiring works by Gluck, Offenbach, and Ravel. Of these, the most powerfully imaginative treatment is Ravel's in his 'symphonie chorégraphique' *Daphnis et Chloé* (1912). Today, Ravel's two orchestral suites of music from this ballet are more often given than the ballet itself: the *Danse guerrière*, *Lever du jour*, and *Danse générale* are well-loved items in the concert-hall. Longus would not, surely, have been displeased at these sumptuous and colourful transformations of a story in which music and dance play an essential part.

[25] Tomas Hägg, *The Novel in Antiquity* (Oxford, 1983), 214–17.

[26] See Paul Ioannides, 'Titian's *Daphnis and Chloe*: A Search for the Subject of a Familiar Masterpiece', in *Apollo*, 133: 352 (June 1991), 374–82. I am obliged to Mr Roger Tarr for drawing my attention to this article. Titian's picture antedates the publication of the first translation and the first Greek text. But Ioannides points out (p. 378) that Titian knew Pietro Bembo, Politian's pupil, and Politian had seen the Florentine manuscript of *Daphnis and Chloe*.

[27] Ibid. 378–82.

NOTE ON THE TEXT AND TRANSLATION

Ancient books were handwritten, and it was in the form of manuscripts that they were handed down through the centuries which
separated late antiquity from the Italian Renaissance. The text of
Daphnis and Chloe is constituted out of two manuscripts, the
thirteenth-century Florentinus Laurentianus Conventi Soppressi
627 (denoted by the letter F, formerly A), and the sixteenth-
century Vaticanus Graecus 1348 (called V, formerly B). F contains three other Greek romances in addition to *Daphnis and
Chloe*. These are *Leucippe and Cleitophon* by Achilles Tatius,
Antheia and Habrocomes by Xenophon of Ephesus, and *Chaereas
and Callirhoë* by Chariton of Aphrodisias. F has no known
descendants, and by itself forms one branch of the manuscript
tradition. V contains, besides *Daphnis and Chloe*, the *Leucippe and
Cleitophon* of Achilles Tatius. It was written in part by a known
scribe, Zacharias Callierges, a Greek working in Italy soon after
the beginning of the sixteenth century. V has numerous descendants, written in the sixteenth century and later, but these have no
independent value as evidence for the text, since they reproduce
the text of V. V and its descendants form the other branch of the
manuscript tradition.[1]

Although V is later than F, it was not copied from F. This is
proved by the fact that V does not transmit a portion of the text
of Book 1, extending from after ἀνέβη ταῖς in 1.12 to before
ἐγένετο at the end of 1.17 (in my translation, approximately
from 'Daphnis came swarming up' to 'when she was not there').
F, on the other hand, transmits the complete text at this point. It
is clear that the writer of V did not have F before him.

Consequently F and V are both regarded as having authority,
independently of each other, as evidence for the text. Where they

---

[1] A fourteenth-century manuscript, *Olomucensis* I VI 9, has four brief extracts from
Daphnis and Chloe and sixteen extracts from *Leucippe and Cleitophon*. This manuscript is
regarded as an earlier representative of the same branch of the tradition as V. See
Longus: Daphnis et Chloe, ed. Michael D. Reeve (Teubner, Leipzig, 1982; 2nd edn. 1986;
3rd edn. 1994), Praefatio VII.

differ from each other, editors adopt the reading of either as they judge preferable, or have recourse to emendation. V is generally more careful and accurate than F. In some places, the text offered by F seems to be the result of clumsy reworking rather than accidental miscopying. The correct explanation of this is doubtless the one proposed by M. D. Reeve: the scribes felt at liberty to alter the text of *Daphnis and Chloe* because they did not consider it to be serious literature.[2] Nevertheless, F sometimes has a better reading than V. Where F and V agree, their agreement is not invariably a sign of correctness.

The first post-Renaissance edition of *Daphnis and Chloe* (the *editio princeps*) was printed at Florence by Philip Junta in 1598. This edition was edited for Junta by Raphael Columbanius, who based the text on a manuscript in the tradition of V, and did not use F. F had been known to Politian in the late fifteenth century and to H. Stephanus in the mid-sixteenth century, but it was thereafter disregarded until Paul-Louis Courier used it for his edition published at Rome in 1810. Courier was the first editor to fill the lacuna at 1.12–17, having found the complete text in F. When he made his copy of these chapters, Courier wrote to the dictation of Francesco Del Furia and the Abbé Bencini, respectively Librarian and Sub-librarian of the Laurentian Library, who could read the crabbed and faded script more readily than he. In the course of further work on the manuscript, he somehow brought an ink-smeared paper into contact with the page which contained the greater part of the newly recovered chapters, blotting out some of the text.[3] Chemical reagents were applied, but without success. The illegible words have consequently to be read in Courier's copy and in two versions written by Bencini after the catastrophe.

A comprehensive account of the textual transmission of *Daphnis and Chloe* can be found in Reeve's preface to the Teubner text.

---

[2] Ibid. Praef. XI.

[3] What exactly happened was obscure from the beginning. See *Paul-Louis Courier, Correspondance générale*, ed. G. Viollet-le-Duc (Paris, 1978), ii. 151–70, 217–23, with pls. III–V. In his diary for 10 Nov. 1809, the day of the incident, Courier notes laconically 'pâté [ink-blot] sur le Longus' (ibid., p. viii).

This is the text that I have translated, except in the following places, where I have preferred a different reading or emendation:

1.1   Translate διακοσίων F instead of εἴκοσιν V.

1.4   Delete καὶ κάλαμοι, with West.

2.34   Delete καὶ after νοεῖ (with Villoison) and reject Reeve's insertion of ἐμπνεῖ.

3.4   Reject Schäfer's insertion of καὶ νυκτερινάς.

3.6   Translate μεριμνῶν VF instead of περιμένων Reeve.

3.29   Translate συρίζειν VF instead of θερίζειν Kairis.

3.32   Translate ἐὰν ταῦτα οὕτως V (lacking in F) instead of Reeve's conjectural reconstruction ἂν ταῦτα ἀληθῆ φανῇ (καὶ γένοιτο οὕτως).

3.33   Translate ἐπέττετο (Korais, cf. *Odyssey* 7.119) instead of ἐπέτετο V (lacking in F) or ἐπέκειτο Villoison, Reeve.

4.20   Translate καθημένης VF instead of ἀποκαθημένης Jungermann.

4.39   Translate the words οὕτως (om. V) αὐτοῖς καὶ ταῦτα συνεγήρασεν. οὗτοι VF, which Reeve deletes following Hercher.

Some passages of my translation are printed with indented margins. This arrangement is not original to the manuscripts, but has been adopted in order to illustrate the elaborately rhetorical structure of these passages. See Introduction, pp. xx–xxii.

CHRONOLOGICAL NOTE

In view of the inconclusive nature of the evidence for dating Longus,[1] I confine myself to a brief account of the period from the middle of the second to the middle of the third centuries AD, within which he is usually assumed to have lived.

The peace and stability which the Roman Empire had enjoyed under the Antonine emperors ended with the death of Antoninus Pius in AD 161. His successor, Marcus Aurelius, soon had to repel attacks by Germanic tribes from east of the Danube, and a Persian invasion of the Roman client-kingdom of Armenia. The decline of the Roman Empire began now. Although Marcus and subsequent emperors sometimes fought successful campaigns, the pressure in these theatres of war was never-ending. On the Danube and the Rhine it was caused by westward migration, in the east by the ambition of successive Persian kings and their appetite for plunder. This warfare had to be financed by increased taxation; the result was inflation, which grew steadily worse for more than a century, impoverishing people and bankrupting municipalities. The army assumed great importance in politics. Vast numbers of troops were under arms; emperors sought to buy their loyalty with costly distributions of money, but this expedient often failed, and there were repeated assassinations and rebellions. Roads, fortifications, and walls were built. All this could not prevent the surrender of territory: tribesmen were allowed to settle on the Roman side of the Danube as early as the reign of Marcus Aurelius, while by 200 southern Scotland had been abandoned to the Caledones. Some emperors were resolute and competent. Such were Marcus Aurelius (161–80), Septimius Severus (193–211), Maximinus I (235–8), Gordian III (238–44), and Philip the Arab (244–9). But there were contrary examples. Commodus (180–92) believed himself to be the reincarnation of Hercules, and would have fought in the arena as a gladiator had

---

[1] See above, pp. viii, xxii.

he not been assassinated first. Elagabalus (218–22) built temples
at Rome for the Syrian sun-god Elagabal, and officiated at the
god's midsummer festival as his high priest. The debauchery
practised by Elagabalus outraged even the Romans. The story of
these hundred years can be followed in the first ten chapters of
Gibbon's *Decline and Fall*, supplemented by the modern
authorities listed in the Select Bibliography.

In literature, only *Daphnis and Chloe* and the *Metamorphoses* of
Apuleius are of outstanding merit at this time: it was not an age
of masterworks. But there was no lack of vitality, and the tradition of scholarship and criticism descending from Hellenistic
Alexandria and Augustan Rome was still unbroken. (In what follows, I mention only works written in Greek.) The period produced a lively satirist in Lucian of Samosata (*fl.* 170), a notable
biographer in the second Philostratus (*fl.* 200, celebrated for his
Lives of the Sophists and *Life of Apollonius of Tyana*), a historian
of importance in Dio Cassius (*fl.* 220), a popularizing writer on
natural history in Aelian (*fl.* 200), an authoritative medical writer
in Galen (*fl.* 170), an orator of surpassing eloquence in Aelius
Aristides (*fl.* 170), and an influential theorist of rhetoric in
Hermogenes (*fl.* 180). The correspondence between the precepts
of Hermogenes and the style of *Daphnis and Chloe* has already
been noted.[2] Achilles Tatius of Alexandria, the author of *Leucippe
and Cleitophon*, probably lived in this period; Longus shares some
structural elements with him,[3] as well as many turns of phrase. In
philosophy, the meditations (*To Himself*) noted down by the
emperor Marcus Aurelius while campaigning on the Danube
show the private and personal side of later Stoicism; of a higher
order of magnitude are the writings of the neoplatonist Plotinus
(*fl.* 250), which expound a whole philosophic system.

At this period Christianity was still a sect, and Christians did
not form a large proportion of the population. They worshipped
in house-churches, and lived in continual expectation of the Second Coming of Christ. Their steadfast refusal to sacrifice to the
emperor, whenever it was brought to the notice of the authorities,

---

[2] See above, pp. xx f.
[3] See above, pp. xi f.

was punished with death. Several emperors instituted persecutions, of which the worst was the one under Decius and his successors, from 251 to 259. After that, the Christians were left in peace until the end of the century.

As Christianity made progress among the upper classes, Christian writers emerged who were equal in culture to their pagan contemporaries. This development took place in Alexandria, where the school for educating new converts in the doctrines of Christianity was headed successively by Clement of Alexandria (150–c.216) and Origen of Alexandria (c.185–254). Clement has a particularly engaging manner: learned, discursive, humane. He shares with Longus an appreciation of Greek comedy and an enthusiasm for the instruction of the neophyte. A curious product of the Christian literature of this time is the sermon on the Passover delivered by Melito, the martyr-bishop of Sardis, a contemporary of Marcus Aurelius. It is composed of balanced clauses and phrases, in a style related to that employed by Longus in his passages of poetic prose[4] and derived from the Gorgianic/Asian school of oratory. For what it is worth, I offer the conjecture that Longus was a contemporary of Melito and Clement.

[4] See above, pp. xx–xxii.

SELECT BIBLIOGRAPHY

A full bibliography for the years 1950–95 is given in J. R. Morgan, 'Longus, *Daphnis and Chloe*: A Bibliographical Survey, 1950–1995', *Aufstieg und Niedergang der römischen Welt*, II, 34, 3 (Berlin, 1997), 2208–76.

Modern Editions and Commentaries

G. Dalmeyda (Budé; Paris, 1934; 2nd edn. 1960; 3rd edn. 1971).

M. D. Reeve (Teubner; Leipzig, 1982; 2nd edn. 1986; 3rd edn. 1994).

O. Schönberger (Berlin, 1960; 2nd edn. 1973; 3rd edn. 1980; 4th edn. 1989).

J.-R. Vieillefond (Paris, 1987).

Translations in English

C. Gill, in B. P. Reardon (ed.), *Collected Ancient Greek Novels* (Berkeley, Los Angeles and London, 1989), 285–348.

J. Lindsay (London, 1948).

G. Moore (London, 1927).

G. Thornley, rev. J. M. Edmonds, with *Parthenius and other fragments*, tr. S. Gaselee (Loeb; Cambridge, Mass. and London, 1916; repr. 1924, 1935, 1955, 1962, 1978).

P. Turner (Penguin; Harmondsworth, 1956; rev. 1968, 1989).

The Ancient Romances

G. Anderson, *Eros Sophistes: Ancient Novelists at Play* (Chico, Calif., 1982).

—— *Ancient Fiction: The Novel in the Graeco-Roman World* (London, 1984).

E. L. Bowie, 'The Greek Novel', in *The Cambridge History of Classical Literature*, vol. I (Cambridge, 1985), 683–99.

—— and S. J. Harrison, 'The Romance of the Novel', *Journal of Roman Studies*, 83 (1993), 159–78.

Margaret Anne Doody, *The True Story of the Novel* (London, 1997).

T. Hägg, *The Novel in Antiquity* (Oxford, 1983).

A. Heisermann, *The Novel Before the Novel* (Chicago and London, 1977).

R. Merkelbach, *Roman und Mysterium in der Antike* (Munich, 1962).

B. E. Perry, *The Ancient Romances: A Literary-Historical Account of their Origins* (Berkeley and Los Angeles, 1967).

B. P. Reardon, *Courants littéraires grecs des IIᵉ et IIIᵉ siècles après J.-C.* (Paris, 1971).

—— (ed.), *Erotica Antiqua: Acta of the International Conference on the Ancient Novel* (Bangor, 1976).

—— *The Form of Greek Romance* (Princeton, 1991).

E. Rohde, *Der griechische Roman und seine Vorläüfer* (Leipzig, 1914; repr. Hildesheim and New York, 1974).

R. Turcan, 'Le roman "initiatique": à propos d'un livre récent', *Revue de l'histoire des religions*, 163 (1963), 149–99.

Language and Style

J. D. Denniston, *Greek Prose Style* (Oxford, 1952).

E. Norden, *Die antike Kunstprosa vom VI. Jahrhundert v. Chr. bis in die Zeit der Renaissance* (Leipzig, 1898; repr. Darmstadt, 1958), i. 126–52, 434–42.

W. Rhys Roberts, *Dionysius of Halicarnassus: On Literary Composition* (London, 1910), 51–6.

G. Valley, 'Über den Sprachgebrauch des Longus' (diss., Uppsala, 1926).

G. Zanetto, 'La lingua dei romanzieri greci', *Giornale Italiano di Filologia*, 42 (1990), 233–42.

Criticism and Interpretation of Daphnis and Chloe

A. Billault, 'La nature dans *Daphnis et Chloé*', *Revue des Études Grecques*, 109 (1996), 506–26.

E. L. Bowie, 'Theocritus' seventh Idyll, Philetas and Longus', *Classical Quarterly*, 35 (1985), 67–91.

H. H. O. Chalk, 'Eros and the Lesbian Pastorals of Longus', *Journal of Hellenic Studies*, 80 (1960), 32–51; repr. in H. Gärtner (ed.), *Beiträge zum griechischen Liebesroman* (= Olms *Studien* 20) (Hildesheim and New York, 1984), 388–407; and in B. Effe (ed.), *Theokrit und die griechische Bukolik* (= Wege der Forschung 580) (Darmstadt, 1986), 402–38.

—— 'Longus Revisited', in B. P. Reardon (ed.), *Erotica Antiqua: Acta of the International Conference on the Ancient Novel* (Bangor, 1976), 133–5.

F. C. Christie, 'Longus and the Development of the Pastoral Tradition' (diss., Harvard, 1972).

P. Green, 'Longus, Antiphon, and the Topography of Lesbos', *Journal of Hellenic Studies*, 102 (1982), 210–14.

R. L. Hunter, *A Study of 'Daphnis and Chloe'* (Cambridge, 1983).

B. D. MacQueen, *Myth, Rhetoric and Fiction: A Reading of Longus' 'Daphnis and Chloe'* (Lincoln and London, 1990).

H. J. Mason, 'Longus and the Topography of Lesbos', *Transactions of the American Philological Association*, 109 (1979), 149–63.

—— 'Romance in a Limestone Landscape', *Classical Philology*, 90 (1995), 263–6.

R. Merkelbach, *Die Hirten des Dionysos. Die Dionysos-Mysterien der römischen Kaiserzeit und der bukolische Roman des Longus* (Stuttgart, 1988).

M. Mittelstadt, 'Longus: *Daphnis and Chloe* and Roman Narrative Painting', *Latomus*, 26 (1967), 752–61.

—— 'Bucolic-lyric Motifs and Dramatic Narrative in Longus' *Daphnis and Chloe*', *Rheinisches Museum für Philologie*, 113 (1970), 211–27.

E. M. O'Connor, '"A bird in the bush": The Erotic and Literary Implications of Bucolic and Avian Imagery in Two Related Episodes of Longus' *Daphnis and Chloe*', *Rheinisches Museum für Philologie*, 134 (1991), 393–401.

G. Rhode, 'Longus und die Bukolik', *Rheinisches Museum für Philologie*, 86 (1937), 23–49; repr. in *Studien und Interpretationen* (Berlin, 1963), 91–116.

R. Turcan, 'Βίος βουκολικὸς ou les Mystères de Lesbos', *Göttingische Gelehrte Anzeigen*, 241 (1989), 169–92.

P. Turner, '*Daphnis and Chloe*: An Interpretation', *Greece and Rome*, NS 7 (1960), 117–23.

G. Wojaczek, *Daphnis. Untersuchungen zur griechischen Bukolik* (Meisenheim-am-Glan, 1969).

A. Wouters, 'The εἰκόνες in Longus' *Daphnis and Chloe* IV 39,2: "Beglaubigungsapparat"?' *Sacris Erudiri*, 31 (1989–90), 465–79.

Background: Literary, Religious, Historical, Social

G. Anderson, *The Second Sophistic* (London, 1993).

G. W. Bowersock, *Greek Sophists in the Roman Empire* (Oxford, 1969).

W. Burkert, *Ancient Mystery Cults* (Cambridge, Mass., 1987).

J. Ferguson, *Religions of the Roman Empire* (London, 1970).

E. Gibbon, *The History of the Decline and Fall of the Roman Empire*, ed. J. B. Bury (London, 1909–14).

M. Grant, *The Climax of Rome* (London, 1968).

V. D. Hanson, *The Other Greeks: The Family Farm and the Agrarian Roots of Western Civilization* (New York, 1995).

R. MacMullen, *Paganism in the Roman Empire* (London, 1981).

H. M. D. Parker, *A History of the Roman World from A.D. 138 to 337*, rev. B. H. Warmington (London, 1958).

Guil. Quandt, 'De Baccho ab Alexandri aetate in Asia Minore culto' (diss., Halle, 1912).

E. L. Shields, 'The Cults of Lesbos' (diss., Johns Hopkins, 1917).

R. Turcan, *The Cults of the Roman Empire* (Oxford, 1996); Eng. trans. by Antonia Nevill of *Les Cultes Orientaux dans le monde Romain* (Paris 1989; 2nd edn. 1992).

Further Reading in Oxford World's Classics

Apuleius, *The Golden Ass*, trans. and ed. P. G. Walsh.

Petronius, *The Satyricon*, trans. and ed. P. G. Walsh.

Greek Lyric Poetry, trans. and ed. M. L. West.

DAPHNIS AND CHLOE

PREFACE*

Out hunting in Lesbos,
in a grove sacred to the Nymphs
I saw a sight
whose like, for beauty, I had never seen—
a painting,
a love-story.
The grove, too, was a pretty spot,
with many trees
and flowers
and streams;
for one spring fed them all,
both flowers and trees.
But the painting was more delightful,
for it was a miracle of skill
and showed a love-affair;
and word of it brought many, even from far away,
to beg some favour of the Nymphs
and view the picture.
In it were women in childbirth
and other women wrapping the babes in swaddling-bands;
infants abandoned in the wild,
herd-animals suckling them,
shepherds lifting them up;
then young lovers were exchanging promises—
but there came a pirate-raid
and an enemy invasion.
There was much more,
and all of it concerning love.
And after I had gazed and marvelled,
I felt a longing to write down what the picture told,
and looked about until I found someone to explain it to me.
And then I set to work and completed these four books—
an offering dedicated to Love, the Nymphs and Pan,

and a delightful possession for everyone,
that will
heal the sick
and cheer the desponding,
bring back memories to those who have loved
and give needful instruction to those who have not.
For, depend upon it, no one has escaped Love or ever will escape,
so long as beauty exists and eyes can see.
And now I pray God to make me discreet while I write the story
of experiences not my own.

BOOK 1

1. Mytilene is a city in Lesbos, a big city and a handsome one; for it is divided by canals, along which the sea comes stealing into its heart, and adorned with bridges made of polished white stone—you would think you were looking at an island rather than a city. About two hundred stades* away from the said city of Mytilene there was an estate belonging to a wealthy man, a very splendid property: it had mountains abounding in game, plains fertile in wheat, gentle slopes with vineyards, pastures with flocks, and a long stretch of shore where the sea broke on the softest of sand.

2. A goatherd called Lamon* was grazing his animals on this estate when he found a child being suckled by one of the she-goats. There was a little wood that sheltered a thicket of brambles and a spreading growth of ivy and some soft grass, on which the infant was lying. The she-goat kept running to this wood and often disappeared inside; it was deserting its kid and spending all its time with the baby. Lamon kept an eye on these comings and goings out of pity for the neglected kid; when noon came he followed the she-goat and saw it standing carefully with its legs astride so as not to harm the baby by treading on it with its hooves, while the child sucked the stream of milk as though from its mother's breast. Lamon was understandably surprised; going closer, he found that the baby was male, a lusty, handsome boy, and swaddled round with better coverings than might have been the lot of an abandoned child, for he was wrapped in a little crimson cloak fastened with a golden brooch, and there was also a dagger with an ivory hilt.

3. Lamon's first thought was to leave the baby and take only the recognition-tokens.* But then, conscious of how shameful it would be if he were to show less mercy than even a goat, he waited till it grew dark, and carried them all—tokens and baby and goat—to his wife Myrtale.* She thought it a strange thing for a goat to have human offspring; but he told her the whole story, how he had found the child abandoned, how he had seen it being fed by the goat, how he had been ashamed to leave it to die. Since Myrtale was of the same mind as her husband, they hid the objects which had accompanied the child, called him their own, and entrusted the feeding of him to the she-goat. And, so that the child's name should have something of the herdsman about it, they decided to call him Daphnis.*

4. Two years now elapsed. At the end of this time a shepherd from a neighbouring estate, Dryas* by name, was tending his flock in the pasture when it befell him to make the same discovery and see the same sight as Lamon. There was a cave sacred to the Nymphs—a massive rock, hollow within, curving on the outside. The Nymphs' statues were made of stone; their feet were sandal-less, their arms were bare to the shoulders, and their hair was hanging loosely about their necks; each had a girdle round her waist and a smile on her face; their whole aspect suggested the dance. In the very middle of the cave in the great rock, water spouted up from a spring and ran away in a stream, so that before the cave there lay a sunken meadow where soft grass grew abundantly, nourished by the moisture. Offerings were laid up in the cave, milk-pails and flutes and pan-pipes, dedicated to the Nymphs by shepherds in years past.

5. A ewe from Dryas' flock, which had lambed not long before, took to visiting this grotto, which several times caused Dryas to think that it was lost. Wishing to curb the ewe and restore it to its usual docility, he made a tether by bending a pliant, green switch into the shape of a noose, and went towards the rock, thinking to catch her there. When he drew near, he was taken aback to see the ewe—exactly like a human mother—giving its teat to a baby for a long, generous suck, while the baby uttered not a sound of complaint, but moved its mouth eagerly to each teat in turn; its lips were clean and pure, because the ewe licked its face over with its tongue, whenever the infant had taken enough of its feed. This child was a girl, and there were lying beside it, as beside the other, emblems of its parentage—a gold-embroidered headband, shoes ornamented with gold, and golden ankle-rings.

6. Now, Dryas thought that his discovery was a gift from the Gods, and, taught by the ewe to pity and cherish the infant, he

picked up the baby and held it in the crook of his arm, stowed the
tokens carefully away in his knapsack, and prayed to the Nymphs
that good fortune would attend his adoption of the child who had
been entrusted to their mercy. When it was time for the flock to
be driven home, Dryas went to his cottage, told his wife what he
had seen, and showed her what he had found; he urged her to
look on the child as a daughter, keeping quiet about its origin and
bringing it up as her own. And Nape* (that was his wife's name)
was instantly a mother and loved the child, as though for fear of
being outshone by the ewe; and, to lend countenance to the adoption, she (like Lamon and Myrtale) called it by a name in use
among the shepherds, and that name was Chloe.*

7. These children grew very quickly, and both began to dis-
play beauty of a higher order than that of mere peasants. When
Daphnis was fifteen years of age and Chloe two years less, Dryas
and Lamon had the following dream on the same night: they
seemed to see the Nymphs of the grotto—the one with the
spring, where Dryas had found the baby—and these Nymphs
were handing over Daphnis and Chloe to a haughty and handsome boy, who had wings sprouting from his shoulders and carried a miniature bow and tiny arrows; and the boy touched both
with one and the same arrow, and commanded them henceforth
to tend flocks, Daphnis the goats and Chloe the sheep.

8. After having this dream, Lamon and Dryas were both dis-
appointed that the foundlings were to be no more than shepherds
and goatherds—the objects abandoned with them had seemed to
give promise of a higher destiny, and because of that they had
given the two children a more delicate upbringing than their
station required, and taught them their letters and whatever other
refinements a peasant could aspire to; but they thought it right to
obey the gods concerning those who owed their survival to divine
providence. And so, after each had told the other about his dream,
they went and offered sacrifice in the Nymphs' grotto to the
winged boy, whose name they did not know; and then they sent
Daphnis and Chloe to be shepherds with the flocks, after first
instructing them in every aspect of the trade. They taught them
how to pasture the animals before the middle of the day, how to

do so a second time after the hottest hours had passed, when to
drive them to water, when to drive them home to their night's
rest, which animals they would have to take a stick to, and which
would obey their word of command. Daphnis and Chloe were as
delighted as if they had succeeded to a great kingdom, and they
loved their goats and sheep more dearly than shepherds usually
do—Chloe, because she awarded the credit for saving her life to a
sheep, and Daphnis, because he remembered that a goat had fed
him when he had been left to starve.

9. It was the beginning of spring, and all the flowers—in
woods and meadows and on the mountains—were bursting into
bloom. There was now the humming of bees, the sound of tuneful birds, the leaping of animals lately born in the flocks; lambs
were cavorting on the mountains, in the meadows bees were buzz-
ing, and the bushes resounded with birdsong. With such a
delightful sense of spring all about them, it was natural that these
two young and impressionable people should begin to imitate
what they heard and saw. They sang when they heard the birds
sing, they jumped about nimbly when they saw the lambs skipping, and they gathered flowers in imitation of the bees—some
they threw into each other's laps, some they wove into garlands,
which they gave the Nymphs as offerings.

10. They kept each other company throughout the whole
day's work, herding their flocks close to one another; Daphnis
would often check Chloe's sheep when any of them wandered
away by themselves, and just as often Chloe would make the
bolder of Daphnis' goats come down from dangerous rocks. Now
and again one of the two would even take charge of both flocks
when the other had become engrossed in some plaything. They
played with the things that commonly amuse shepherds and children. Chloe would pick stems of asphodel in one spot or another,
and plait them into a cage for a grasshopper or a cricket*—when
she was busy about this she forgot her sheep. Daphnis would cut
some slender reeds,* bore through their solid joints, fasten them
side-by-side with soft wax, and then practise pan-piping until it
was dark. When mealtimes came, they shared each other's drinks
of milk or wine, and dealt out equally the rations brought from

home. You would sooner have seen the sheep and the goats parted from each other than Chloe and Daphnis.

11. They were passing their time in childish games like these, when Love hatched a scheme that turned their sport to earnest. It came about in this way. A she-wolf with cubs was seizing many animals from other flocks in the neighbouring fields, being in constant need of food to rear her young. And so the country people banded together to go out at night-time and dig pits, measuring one orgyia* across and four deep. They carried away most of the soil which they had dug out, and scattered it at a distance; then they laid long, dry twigs over the hole, and sprinkled the remaining soil on top, to make the ground look as it had before; the result being that if as little as a hare ran across, it would snap the twigs, which were more fragile than straw, and then the victim would know (too late) that the ground was not firm, but had only been made to appear so. They dug many pits like this in the mountains and on the plain, but they did not succeed in catching the wolf: *she* knows when there has been tampering—even with the ground. But the pits were the death of many goats and sheep, and very nearly of Daphnis also, as we shall see.

12. Two billy-goats lost their temper and began to fight; they butted each other so violently that one of them suffered a broken horn, and retreated, snorting with pain. The victor kept hard on the loser's heels, until he had turned its retreat into a rout. Daphnis was annoyed about the broken horn, and he was displeased at such wanton aggression; so he took a stick in one hand and his crook in the other, and pursued the pursuer. With the goat trying to escape and Daphnis angrily running after him, neither was keeping watch on what was ahead—down they went, therefore, into a pit, the goat leading, and Daphnis coming after; this circumstance saved Daphnis, since he had the benefit of the goat to cushion his fall. He could only wait there, weeping with shock, for someone to pull him out—if, that is, a rescuer was at hand. Happily Chloe saw what had happened, ran to the pit, and, finding Daphnis alive, called for help to a cowherd in a nearby field. The cowherd came, and then went to look for a long rope

for Daphnis to hang on to and be hauled up to safety. But no rope could be found; and it was left for Chloe to unwind the broad band of cloth* that bound her bosom and give it to the herdsman to let down into the pit. And then they stood at the edge of the pit and pulled, and Daphnis came swarming up hand-over-hand, following the long breast-band as it rose. They also drew up the wretched goat, whose horns were both broken off; so grievous a penalty did Justice exact from him for his defeat of the other goat. They told the cowherd that he could have him to sacrifice, as a reward for saving Daphnis; if anyone at home missed him, they were going to pretend that wolves had attacked the herd.

They themselves went back and surveyed the flock of sheep and the herd of goats. And after they had made sure that goats and sheep were peacefully grazing, they sat down beneath the trunk of an oak and looked to see whether any part of Daphnis' body was bleeding after his fall. There proved to be no wounds and no blood, but his hair and body were bespattered with earth and mud. He thought that he had better have a bath before Lamon and Myrtale noticed that something untoward had happened.

13. He and Chloe went, therefore, to the grotto of the Nymphs; and then, giving her his tunic and his knapsack to look after, he stepped up to the spring, and washed his hair and all his body. His hair was black and luxuriant, and his body was sunburnt—one could have imagined that it had been tinted golden-brown by the shadow of his hair. As Chloe looked on, it occurred to her that Daphnis was handsome; she had never considered him so before, and that made her think that the bath must be the cause of his beauty. When she helped him to wash his back, the skin felt so soft and yielding beneath her touch that she repeatedly ran her fingers over her own body (unseen by Daphnis) to see whether he had the more exquisite flesh. After that it was nearly sunset, and they drove their flocks homewards. Chloe was left feeling nothing but the desire to see Daphnis bathing again.

When they came to the pasture next day, Daphnis sat down

beneath the familiar oak-tree, played his pan-pipes, and watched over his goats as they lay apparently listening to the melodies. Chloe sat nearby and watched her flock of sheep—but she spent more time looking at Daphnis; as he blew his pipes, she thought again that he was handsome, and, in the same way as before, she supposed that the cause of his beauty was his music-playing. This led her to take the pan-pipes after him, hoping that they would make her beautiful, too. Then she persuaded him to bathe again, and watched him bathing, and passed from watching to touching—and then she went away, but only after she had said something complimentary to him.

That little word of praise was the beginning of love. Chloe did not know what was wrong with herself, young and countrified as she was, and never having so much as heard another person uttering the name of love. A vague feeling of unease possessed her, her eyes seemed to have developed a will of their own, and she talked incessantly about Daphnis. She would not eat, she lay awake at night, she ceased to care about her sheep. She laughed at one moment and cried the next; sat down and jumped up again; turned pale, then flushed fiery red. Even a cow bitten by a gadfly is not as restive as Chloe was.

14. One day, when she was all by herself, the following soliloquy came to her:

'Now I am sick,
  but don't know what with;
I am in pain,
  yet have no wound upon me;
I am unhappy,
  yet none of my sheep has been lost;
I am on fire,
  and yet I am sitting deep in the shade.
How often have brambles scratched me
  without making me weep!
How often have bees stung me
  without making me cry out!
But this feeling that pricks my heart is sharper than all these.

Daphnis is beautiful—
　　why, so are the flowers!
His pan-pipes make sweet music—
　　why, so do the nightingales!
But I don't care for any of *them*.
　　I wish I were his pipes,
　　　　so that he could blow his breath into me.
　　I wish I were a goat,
　　　　so that Daphnis could drive me out to pasture.
Wicked water!
　　you made Daphnis beautiful, and Daphnis only;
　　　　when I washed in you, you did nothing for *my* looks.
Dear Nymphs! I'm going to die—
even you will not save the girl who grew up beneath your care.

　　Who will bring you garlands when I am gone?
　　Who will feed the poor motherless lambs?
　　Who will look after the gossiping cricket
　　that I caught and caged with so much trouble,
for it to sit before the cave and send me to sleep with its voice?

But now I am sleepless because of Daphnis,
and the cricket chatters in vain.'

15. These were Chloe's emotions, and these the words she spoke, as she tried to find the name of love.

But now enter again Dorcon* the cowherd—the same who had hauled Daphnis and the goat out of the trap. He was a young fellow whose beard was just beginning to grow, and he knew the name of love *and* also its deeds. From that day forward he was in love with Chloe, and as time went on his passion grew hotter. Despising Daphnis—who seemed to him only a boy—he made up his mind to get his way by gifts or by violence. He began by bringing them presents. To Daphnis he gave a set of pan-pipes, of the kind that cowherds play; they were made of nine reeds, fastened together with bronze instead of wax. To Chloe he gave the skin of a fawn, as worn in the rites of Dionysus; its colour was as fresh and strong as though it had been painted on. Disarmed by these gifts, they took him for a friend;

but by degrees he disregarded Daphnis, whereas he brought Chloe some new gift every day—a soft cheese, or a garland of flowers, or a ripe apple; once it was a new-born calf, and once a wooden cup decorated with gold, and once a brood of nestlings brought from the mountains.* Chloe had never before encountered a lover's wiles, and so she accepted Dorcon's gifts gladly. But it pleased her more that she had something to give Daphnis.

The time had now come when Daphnis, too, was destined to become acquainted with the deeds of love. One day, he and Dorcon had a contest to decide which of them was the handsomer. They appointed Chloe as judge, and, as a prize, the winner was to be allowed to kiss her. Both made speeches. Dorcon began, and spoke as follows:

16. 'I am taller than Daphnis, maiden, and I am a cowherd, whereas he is a goatherd; and so I am better than Daphnis by the same measure as cattle are better than goats. And I am as white as milk and as auburn-haired as corn ripe for cutting. And I had a mother to bring me up, not a beast. But Daphnis is little, and he has no more hair on his chin than a woman, and he is as black as a wolf. He herds billy-goats, and carries the stink of them around with him, and he is so poor that he can't even afford to keep a dog. And if it's true what they say, that a goat gave him her milk, he's no different from a kid.'

That, and more of the same, was Dorcon's case. Then it was the turn of Daphnis:

'I had a she-goat as my nurse—so did Zeus. I herd goats—bigger goats than Dorcon's cows! But I *don't* smell of them, because Pan doesn't either, although he's three parts goat. I'm content with cheese and a bit of toasted bread and some retsina—a peasant is well off if he has that much. You say that I haven't a beard; well, neither does Dionysus. You say I'm black; well, so are hyacinths. But Dionysus is better than the Satyrs,* and hyacinths are better than lilies. Look at Dorcon—he's as tawny as a fox and as bearded as a billy-goat and as white-skinned as a woman from the town. When you have to kiss the winner, it's my mouth that you'll kiss—whereas you'd be kissing the hairs on Dorcon's chin.

And remember, maiden, a sheep suckled you—but you're beautiful!'

17. At this, Chloe waited no longer; the compliment pleased her, and in any case she had been longing to kiss Daphnis. She jumped up and kissed him—it was a naive and unsophisticated kiss, but it had the power to make any man hot with desire.

Dorcon was mortified, and ran away to look for some other road to love. But as for Daphnis, he behaved as though he had been bitten, not kissed. He immediately began to scowl, and little chills kept running over him, and he could not stop his heart from fluttering. He wanted to look at Chloe, but whenever he did look, he flushed crimson. Then for the first time he was smitten with admiration for her hair, because it was so blonde, and for her eyes, because they were as big as a cow's, and for her face, because it really was whiter than goat's milk—it was as though he possessed eyes for the first time, and had always been blind before. He would not take more than a taste of food, and if he was made to drink, he would do no more than wet his lips. He was silent—Daphnis, who had been more chatty than a cricket! He was idle—Daphnis, who had been more active than a goat! His herd was neglected, his pan-pipes were cast aside, his face was more colourless than grass at high summer.* He would talk to no one but Chloe; and when she was not there, he talked to himself, babbling like a madman:

18.   'What on earth is Chloe's kiss doing to me?
        Her lips were softer than rose-petals,
        her mouth was sweeter than honeycomb,
    but that kiss has caused me more pain than a bee-sting!
        I have often kissed the baby goats,
        I have often kissed new-born puppies,
        and the calf that Dorcon gave;
    but that kiss was something uncanny.
        My breath leaps from me,
        my heart gives a bound,
        my soul is melting away—
    and yet I long to kiss her again.

Oh what a cowardly victory for her!
Oh what an unheard-of ailment for me!—
I can't even give a name to it.
Did Chloe taste poison before kissing me?
If she did, why didn't she die?

Listen to the nightingales singing,
   while my pan-pipes are silent.
Look at the little goats skipping,
   while I'm just sitting here,
and all the flowers blooming,
    but I'm not twisting them into garlands—
the violets and the hyacinths are in full flower,
but Daphnis is withering.*
Will Dorcon look handsomer than me in the end?'

19. That is what our precious Daphnis said and suffered—it was his first taste of the words and actions of people in love. Meanwhile, though, the cowherd Dorcon, who was still Chloe's passionate admirer, watched and waited until he saw Dryas digging in a vine nearby; then he went up to him with some of his best small cheeses, which he insisted on presenting to him—he was an old friend of his, from the days when Dryas had himself been a cowherd. From this beginning he proceeded to open the possibility of marrying Chloe, and promised many splendid gifts (splendid for a cowherd, at any rate) if he were to get her as his wife—a yoke of ploughing-oxen, four hives full of bees, fifty apple trees, a bull's hide for cutting up into shoes, and an annual present of a calf already weaned from its mother. Charmed by these gifts, Dryas came close to giving his consent for the marriage. But he knew that Chloe was worthy of a better bridegroom, and he was afraid that he would have to pay dearly if his blunder ever became known. So he said no to the marriage, begged Dorcon's pardon, and declined to accept the proffered gifts.

20. Thus Dorcon had been cheated of his hope a second time, and had lost good cheeses to no avail. His only chance now, it seemed to him, was to catch Chloe alone and ravish her. By keeping close watch, he discovered that they drove the animals to water day-about, Daphnis taking a turn and then Chloe, and this suggested to him a scheme appropriate for a herdsman. He took the skin of a big wolf which a bull had once gored to death while defending his cows, and draped it round himself so that it hung down his back as far as his feet; its forepaws covered his hands, its rear paws his legs down to the heel, while its gaping jaws sat over his head, just like a soldier's helmet. When he had finished making himself look as much like a beast as he could, he took his way to the spring where the sheep and goats drank after grazing. The spring was in a deep hollow, and all round it there grew a tangled mass of thorns, brambles, low juniper bushes, and thistles. It was the perfect place for a real wolf to lurk in ambush. Dorcon hid himself there and waited for the time when the flocks would come to drink; he was sure that he would get his hands on Chloe after terrifying her with his wolf-suit.

21. A short time passed, and Chloe came, driving both flocks down to the spring—she had left Daphnis cutting green, leafy branches for the kids to nibble after they had been driven home from the pasture. She was followed by the dogs who guarded the sheep and goats, and as they sniffed around in the endlessly inquisitive way that dogs have, they came upon Dorcon just as he was stirring to attack Chloe. Amid a chorus of shrill barks, they hurled themselves on what they took for a wolf, surrounded Dorcon while he was still too astonished to get properly onto his feet, and began to bite savagely. For a moment or two Dorcon continued to lie silently in the bushes—he was ashamed of being exposed, and his wolfskin covering gave him protection. But as for Chloe, one look was enough to frighten her out of her wits, and she began screaming to Daphnis for help, while simultaneously the dogs dragged the wolfskin from Dorcon and got their teeth into his flesh. This was too much for the cowherd. He gave a loud yelp of pain and begged Daphnis and Chloe to rescue him, Daphnis having arrived by this time. They called the dogs off with a few familiar words, and soon had them quiet; and then they turned their attention to Dorcon, who had been bitten about the thighs and shoulders. They led him to the spring, washed his lacerations, and sprinkled them over with green elm-bark,* which they first chewed in order to soften it. Daphnis and Chloe did not know the lengths to which frustrated lovers will go, and were inclined to regard Dorcon's wearing of the wolfskin as merely a herdsman's idea of fun; and so they were not angry with him at all, but actually tried to cheer him up, and took his hand for a few steps on his road home, after which they left him to make his own way.

22. It had been a close shave for Dorcon—he had escaped not from the proverbial 'wolf's mouth'* but from the dog's—and now he lay low and doctored his wounds. Meanwhile, Daphnis and Chloe were kept busy until nightfall, collecting together the scattered sheep and goats. The poor creatures had panicked at the sight of the wolfskin, and the barking of the dogs had increased their confusion; the goats had gone scampering up onto the rocks, while the sheep had run down to the sea, and even into the water. They had been trained to obey the word of command, just as they had learned to surrender to the spell of the pan-pipes and to come together at the sound of a hand-clap; now, however, fear made them forget all that, and Daphnis and Chloe had a hard job to get them back to the farmyard, following their hoof-prints as though they were tracking hares. On that night and that night alone they both slept deeply and found in their hard work a cure for the pain of love. But next morning their torment began all over again—they were glad to meet, and sad to part; they wanted something, but could not tell what it was. This only they knew, that Chloe's kiss had unmanned Daphnis, and Daphnis bathing had undone Chloe.

23. Their flames were fanned by the season of the year. It was now the end of spring and the beginning of summer, and all creation was burgeoning; the trees were hung with fruits, the corn was standing high in the plains; pleasant was the sound made by the cicadas, sweet the fragrance of the ripe fruit, gladsome the bleating of the flocks; you would have thought that the rivers were singing as they rippled gently past, and that the sough of the wind among the pines was the moan of pan-pipes, and that the ripe apples dropping to the ground were yielding to a lover, and that the sun was making everyone disrobe because he liked to

spy on beauty. All this had the effect of inflaming Daphnis and making him wade into the rivers—sometimes he bathed, sometimes he chased after the fish as they flickered and twirled through the water, and often he drank, to quench the blaze inside him. Chloe had to milk the ewes and most of the nanny-goats, and after that she had a long and wearisome task churning the milk, because the flies were a dreadful nuisance and liable to bite if they were not continually driven away. But when she had finished and had washed her face, she would put a crown of pine-sprigs on her head, and dress herself in the fawn-skin, which she wore with a belt. Then she would fill her pail with wine and milk, and share it with Daphnis.

24. Then it would be the hour of noon, and that was the time when their eyes were captivated. For Chloe caught the full impact of Daphnis' beauty when she saw him naked from bathing, and her heart melted within her, because every part of his body was perfection; while the sight of Chloe wearing her pine-crown and her fawn-skin and holding out the pail to him made Daphnis think that he was looking at one of the Nymphs of the cave. He could not resist snatching the pine-crown from Chloe's head and putting it on his own, after first planting a kiss on it; in retaliation, Chloe picked up his clothes while he was naked in the water and dressed herself in them, kissing them first, as he had done. Now and again they indulged in an apple-fight, or invented fancy coiffures, separating each other's hair into braids; Chloe told Daphnis that his hair was like myrtle-berries, it was so black, and he said that her face was like an apple, because it was white with a hint of pink. Daphnis also taught Chloe how to play his pan-pipes; but every time that she began to blow on them, he would snatch them away and run his own lips over the reeds—he pretended to be correcting her mistakes, but he was really using the pipes as a way of kissing Chloe without doing anything unseemly.

25. Once at midday Daphnis was playing his pipes and the animals were lying in the shade, when Chloe nodded off into a doze. At first Daphnis did not notice. But when he did, he put down his pipes and gazed at her sleeping body from head to

foot—he looked long and greedily, for there was nothing to make him feel guilty at taking such an advantage. As he bent over her, he murmured softly to himself:

'What heavenly eyes are sleeping! What a paradise breathes from her mouth! apples and pears are not as sweet-scented. But I shan't risk kissing her—kisses bite your heart, and they can drive you mad, just like new honey. And I'm afraid that I'll wake her up if I kiss her. Listen to those chattering cicadas—they won't let her sleep with their rasping! And there go the billy-goats clashing their horns together in battle—what cowards the wolves are, worse than foxes, for not snatching them away by now! . . .'

26. Daphnis was in mid-utterance when suddenly a cicada landed in Chloe's bosom—it was fleeing from a swallow, which was trying to snap it up. The swallow still pursued, and although it could not catch the cicada, in giving chase it flew so near to Chloe that it brushed her cheeks with its wings. Not knowing what was happening, she started out of her sleep with a loud cry. When she saw the swallow circling nearby and Daphnis laughing at her panic, she stopped being afraid, and began to rub her eyes, which would have preferred to be still asleep—whereupon the cicada sounded from her bosom, like a suppliant returning thanks for his preservation. This caused Chloe to let out another shriek; Daphnis burst out laughing, and availed himself of the excuse to slide his hands down over her breasts and draw forth the gallant cicada. Even when held in his hand the insect continued to chirp. Chloe was charmed when she saw the cicada; she took it and kissed it, then popped it back—still chattering—into her bosom.

27. One day they were enjoying the pastoral lilt of a wood-pigeon calling from the wood. Chloe was curious to know what it was saying, and Daphnis became her teacher; he recounted to her this legend which has been told for generations:

'There once was a girl as pretty as you, girl, and she used to herd cows, as many as yours, in a wood. This girl, you must know, was also a good singer, and her cows loved her music—her way of herding them was not to beat them with a stick or prod them with a goad, but she would simply sit down beneath a pine-tree,

garland herself with sprigs of pine, then sing the song about Pan
and Pitys the pine-tree nymph, and the cows always kept close to
her voice. There was a boy who pastured cows not far away, and
he was as handsome as the girl was pretty, and he could sing just
as well as she. This boy set up as her rival at singing, and he
displayed a voice that was louder than hers, because he was a
male, but sweet, because he was a boy. He succeeded in fascinat-
ing the best eight cows in her herd and luring them away into his
own. The girl was desolated because of the loss to her herd and
the defeat of her singing, and she prayed to the gods to be turned
into a bird before she reached home again. The gods granted her
prayer: they made her the bird you hear now, a mountain-dweller,
like the girl, and a music-maker, like her, and to this day she still
proclaims her misfortune in song, telling everyone that she is
searching for her stray cows.'

28. Those were the amusements that summer afforded them.
But when autumn had come and the grapes were beginning to
darken, pirates made an attack on the coast. They came from
Pyrrha,* but they were using a Carian *hemiolia** in order to pass
themselves off as foreigners. Putting in close to the cultivated
fields, they came ashore armed with swords and wearing breastplates, and proceeded to carry off whatever came to hand, including fragrant wine,* a vast amount of wheat, and honey in the
comb. They also drove away some cows from Dorcon's herd.
Daphnis, too, was captured as he walked idly near the sea*—
Chloe was always later in driving Dryas' sheep afield, because she
was a girl and afraid of being bullied by the other shepherds.
When the pirates saw that they had got hold of a youth who was
tall and handsome and worth more than the booty to be found in
the fields, they did not waste time rounding up his goats or plundering the rest of the neighbourhood, but led Daphnis down to
their ship, weeping and helpless and crying out loudly to Chloe.
The pirates untied the mooring-rope and dipped their oars into
the water, and they were just heading out to sea when Chloe came
driving her flock down to the shore and bringing new pan-pipes
as a gift for Daphnis. When she saw that the goats were in dis-
order and heard Daphnis calling her name ever more and more

frantically, she forgot about her sheep, threw down the pipes, and ran to Dorcon to ask for his help.

29. But Dorcon lay weltering in blood and scarcely breathing—the pirates had cut him down with vicious blows. He saw Chloe, and felt a glow from the embers of his old passion.

'Chloe,' he whispered, 'I'm not long for this world. I tried to defend the herd, but those wicked pirates butchered me like one of my own cattle. Please, Chloe, save Daphnis and avenge me and destroy them. I taught my cows to follow the pipes and come towards their song, even when they were grazing in a far-off pasture. Come on, then—take my pipes and play that tune that I once taught Daphnis, and he taught you; the pipes and the cows on the ship will do the rest. I want you to keep the pipes—they're the ones that I beat scores of cowherds and goatherds with, when I used to compete. In return for them, kiss me while I still live, and weep for me when I die. And when you see someone else pasturing my cows, remember me.'

30. So Dorcon spoke his last words and kissed his last kiss and gave up the ghost, even while he spoke and kissed. But Chloe took the pipes and put them to her lips and piped her loudest. The cows heard her and recognized the tune—they bellowed loudly, and then jumped with one impulse into the sea. This violent movement to one side, and the trough made in the waves where the cattle had plunged in, caused the ship to heel over; next moment the water came surging back, and the ship was engulfed and its occupants washed overboard. They did not all have the same chance of survival, however. For the pirates were girded with their swords and encased in their breastplates of metal scales, and they had greaves fastened to their legs below the knee, whereas Daphnis was shoeless, because he did his herding on smooth ground, and he was lightly clad, because the weather was still hot. So the pirates were carried to the bottom by the weight of their armour, after swimming for only a short time. Daphnis, on the other hand, slipped out of his clothes easily enough, but the effort of swimming tired him, since he had only swum in rivers before. Soon, though, Necessity taught him what had to be done; and he swam into the midst of the cows, seized with each

hand a horn of each of two cows, and was carried along between
them with as little trouble and effort as if he were driving a
wagon.* It must here be observed that the ox is a stronger swim-
mer than man, and is surpassed only by water-fowl and, of
course, fish; a swimming ox cannot drown, unless the horn of its
hooves becomes saturated and drops off. The many areas of the
sea still named Oxen-fords bear witness to this tale.

31. In this way, then, Daphnis was saved, and he escaped the
double danger, of piracy and shipwreck, after his plight had
seemed hopeless. When he emerged from the sea, Chloe was
standing on the beach, laughing and crying, and he fell into her
arms. Then, in answer to his question why she had sounded the
pipes, she related the whole story—her dash to Dorcon, Dorcon's
former schooling of the cows, how he had told her to pipe, and
his death. The only thing she left out was the kiss, which it
embarrassed her to think about.

Needless to say, they resolved to pay proper respect to their
late benefactor, and accordingly they went and helped Dorcon's
relatives to bury the poor fellow. They heaped a big mound of
earth over him, and planted it generously with cultivated trees
and shrubs, on which they hung some of their produce from the
fields, as offerings to the dead man. They also poured milk and
squeezed grape-juice onto the grave, and broke in pieces above it
many sets of pan-pipes. A sorrowful noise of lowing was heard
coming from the cattle, and, simultaneously with the lowing,
strange and aimless rushings to-and-fro were noted, which led
the shepherds and the goatherds to aver that the cattle were
lamenting for their dead master.*

32. When Dorcon's funeral was over, Chloe took Daphnis to
the cave of the Nymphs, and led the way inside. First she helped
him to wash; then it was her turn, and that was the first time that
she took a bath with Daphnis looking on. Her body was white and
pure—this was a natural feature of her beauty, and she had no
need of baths to make her beautiful. Then they gathered the
flowers of that season, put garlands on the statues, and hung up
Dorcon's pipes on the rocky wall of the cave, as an offering to
the Nymphs. After that they went and inspected the goats and the

sheep. All were lying on the ground, and were not grazing or bleating—I think they were missing Daphnis and Chloe, who had been out of sight all this time. Certainly when the pair reappeared and called out and played their pipes as usual, the sheep stood up and began to feed, while the goats skipped and snorted as if in delight at the preservation of their accustomed master.

Daphnis, though, could not bring himself to rejoice, because he had seen Chloe naked, and beauty had been revealed to his eyes which had always been concealed before. His heart ached as though it were being eaten by poison, and sometimes his breath burst forth violently, as if he were being chased, while sometimes it died away, as if it had all been used up in his recent adventures. Chloe bathing, he thought to himself, was more to be feared than the sea; and he felt as though his life yet lay in pirate hands. For he was young and country-bred, and he still knew nothing of the piracy of Love.

BOOK 2

1. Now it was well and truly autumn, and the grape-harvest was fast approaching. All the country-people were hard at work; one man was repairing the wine-presses, another was scrubbing out the storage-jars, another was weaving baskets; a fourth was busy with his little sickle for cutting the bunches of grapes, a fifth was looking for a stone heavy enough to squeeze the last drops of juice from the spent grapes, and a sixth was making bundles of dry withies,* which had been pounded and shredded for use as torches, so that there would be light for conveying the grape-juice after dark.* Daphnis and Chloe took time off from their goats and sheep, and lent a hand where it was needed. Daphnis carried baskets of grapes, emptied them into the wine-press, and stayed to tread them; then he helped to carry the wine and pour it into the jars. Chloe prepared food for the grape-pickers, and kept them supplied with drinks of older wine. She also harvested the vines that were closest to the ground. All the vines on Lesbos, you see, are low-growing;* they are not raised on trellises or supported on trees, but put out their branches in a downward direction and spread like ivy—even an infant whose hands were newly out of its swaddling-bands would be able to reach the grapes.

2. There is bound to be some licence at a festival celebrating Dionysus and the discovery of wine, and, sure enough, the local women brought in to help with the vintage were soon casting a saucy eye on Daphnis; they made up to him by saying that he was as handsome as Dionysus himself, and one of the bolder ones even kissed him—which excited Daphnis, but upset Chloe. The score was evened when the men trampling in the vats called out various ribaldries to Chloe, and leapt up with redoubled frenzy, like Satyrs bidding for the favours of a Bacchante,* and prayed to be changed into sheep and be herded by her—that was Chloe's cue to feel complacent, but Daphnis suffered a pang. The effect of all this was to make them pray for a speedy end to the vintage,

so that they might return to their familiar haunts and have in their ears the pan-pipes or the bleating of their flocks instead of crude and witless bawling. And when, after a few more days, the vines had all been stripped and the jars held their store of new wine and there was no longer any need for extra workers, Daphnis and Chloe drove their flocks down to the plain again, and went joyfully to prostrate themselves before the Nymphs, bringing them some bunches of grapes still hanging from the branch, as first-fruits of the vintage. It had never been their custom, previously, to pass by the grotto without some mark of respect, but they would always present themselves to the Nymphs when they began the day's grazing and bow down to them when they were coming home at night, and they never failed to bring them an offering—a flower or a fruit or a green bough or a cup of milk poured reverently for the Nymphs to drink. In due course their assiduity was rewarded by the goddesses. But for the present they were (to coin a phrase) like puppies let off the leash—they gambolled, piped, sang, and wrestled with their goats and sheep.

3. Their fun was in full swing when it was interrupted by the arrival of an old man; he was wearing a hairy goatskin, his shoes were brogues made of untanned hide, and round him was slung a leather bag which was as venerable as its owner. He sat down close to them and began to speak:

'My dear children! Old Philetas* am I, who sang many a song to the Nymphs here,* and piped many a tune to Pan yonder,* and led a big herd of cattle where I would by the power of music alone. I have come to declare to you the sight that I saw and to make known to you the tidings that I heard.

'I have a garden that I tend with my own hands—it has been my pride and joy ever since I gave up being a cowherd because of old age. All things that the Seasons bring forth, this garden bears in each several season. In spring there are roses and white lilies and hyacinths and both kinds of violets, in summer poppies and wild pears and every sort of apple, and at the present season grapes and figs and pomegranates and green myrtle-berries. Every morning flocks of birds foregather in this garden, some to feed, some to sing; for the trees make a canopy overhead, and there is pleasant shade, and water comes from three springs; take away the boundary-wall, and you would think that you were looking at a woodland grove.

4. 'I went into my garden today about noon, and what did I see there under the pomegranate-trees and myrtle-bushes but a boy with his hands full of myrtle-berries and pomegranates. His skin was as white as milk, his hair was as yellow as flame, and he was as radiant as though he had just come from his bath. Naked he was, and all alone; and he was disporting himself as though the garden were his to take what he liked from. Well, I started forward, meaning to lay hold of him, because I was afraid that the young scamp would break down my myrtles and pomegranates. But he was too nimble on his feet for me, and he easily got away—now he dodged under the rose-bushes, now he vanished under the poppies, slipping from covert to covert like a partridge-chick. I don't mind telling you that I've often had my work cut out chasing the unweaned kids, and I've often wearied my legs running after a frisky young calf; but this was a wily creature, and he was not to be caught. I'm an old man, and I soon grew tired; so I halted, leaned on my staff, and—taking care not to let him escape—asked him which of the neighbours was his father and what he meant by taking fruit from someone else's garden. He spoke not a word in answer, but came quite near to me and gave the most delicious laugh—then he pelted me with myrtle-berries, and somehow charmed away my anger. I found myself begging him not to be afraid, but to come into my arms, and I swore by these same myrtle-berries that I would let him go with a gift of apples and pomegranates and that I would always allow him to strip the fruit-trees and pluck the flowers—if only he would let me have one kiss.

5. 'Again came that indescribably musical laugh, and then he spoke in such a voice as neither swallow has nor nightingale nor the swan who sings because he is as old as I: "For me to kiss you, Philetas, is no hardship, no hardship at all; because I want to be kissed more than you want to be young again. But consider

whether that favour would suit your time of life—one kiss from me, and even your old age will not avail to save you from everlasting pursuit of me! A difficult prey to catch am I for hawk and eagle and any swifter bird than they! I am no boy, though boy is what I seem, but I am older than Cronos and all Time itself; I know that, in the heyday of your youth, you grazed your far-spreading herd of cattle* on the mountain yonder, and I was with you while you played your pan-pipes near the oak-trees there, what time you were in love with Amaryllis, but you did not see *me*, although I was standing very close to her. And so I gave her to be yours, and today your sons are sturdy cowherds and yeomen. But Daphnis and Chloe are my sheep now, and after I have brought them together every morning I come into your garden and enjoy the flowers and trees, and bathe in these springs. That is why your garden grows so thrivingly—the flowers and trees take their water from my bath! And now be off, and look whether any of your trees is broken or any of your fruit taken or any flower-root trodden on or any spring made muddy! And so farewell to you, who alone of men have been granted a sight of this boy in your old age!"

6. 'With these words he leapt up into the myrtles like a fledgeling nightingale, and went from branch to branch through the leaves until he came to the top. I saw wings on his shoulders and a tiny bow and arrows between the wings—and then of him and them no trace. Now, if my grey hairs have not come to me in vain, and if my wits have not been addled by my years, I say that you have been consecrated to Love, dear children, and Love is watching over you.'

7. Daphnis and Chloe were as delighted as if they had been listening to some charming fantasy instead of a true story; and they asked Philetas what kind of being Love was—whether boy or bird—and what powers he possessed. And so Philetas began afresh:

'My dear children! Love is a god, and he is young and fair, and he can fly. And so he takes pleasure in all youth and seeks out beauty and causes souls to grow wings. As for his powers, he has such power as even Zeus has not:*

'Love rules the elements,
Love rules the stars,
Love rules the gods, his peers—
his sway over them exceeds yours over your goats and sheep.
All flowers are the works of Love,
all trees are his creations;
through his power
do rivers flow,
and winds blow.
I have known a bull to be in love,
and he bellowed as though a gadfly had stung him;
and I have seen a billy-goat that loved a nanny-goat,
and he went about after her everywhere.
I was once young myself and fell in love with Amaryllis,
and I could neither think of food
nor swallow drink
nor take rest—
I ached in spirit,
my heart fluttered,
my body grew chill;
I cried out as though beneath the lash,
I was as silent as a corpse,
I plunged into rivers as if I burned;
I called to Pan for succour because he had loved
Pitys,
I heaped praise on Echo because she sang out the name of
Amaryllis after me,
I broke my pan-pipes because, although they charmed my
cows, they did not bring me Amaryllis.
For there is no remedy for Love,*
no cure to be drunk
or eaten
or chanted in spells,
save only
kissing
and embracing
and lying down naked together.'

8. After he had taught them thus, Philetas took his leave, though not before he had received a gift of several cheeses and a kid whose horns were already growing. Left alone, and having then for the first time heard the name of Love, Daphnis and Chloe were chastened in spirit and uneasy. Night came, and they parted and went home to their separate cottages. And then they fell to comparing their own feelings with what Philetas had told them:

'Lovers feel pain—why, so do we! They neglect their food—just as we have done! They can't sleep—that's just our difficulty now! They think they're burning—there's fire in us, too! They long for the sight of each other—that's why we pray for day to come more quickly! Maybe this is Love, and we are in love with each other without knowing it—or else it's Love, but it's only I who feel it. But if that's so, why do we both feel the same pain? And why are we so eager for each other's company? It must all be true, what Philetas said! The little boy that he saw in his garden was seen by our fathers too, in that dream that they both had, and he commanded that we should pasture the flocks. How can he be caught? He's little, and he'll escape. How can he *be* escaped? He has wings and he'll catch us. I know!—we'll have to flee to the Nymphs, and they'll help us.—Oh no they won't, for Pan didn't help Philetas either, when he was in love with Amaryllis. So we must take the medicine that Philetas told us about: kissing, embracing, and lying naked on the ground. It'll be cold, but we'll grin and bear it, as Philetas did before us!'

9. These night-thoughts were an education to them both, and when the next day came and they drove their flocks to pasture, they kissed on meeting—something that they had not done previously—and embraced so closely that the arms of each were crossed behind the other's back. But they shrank from the third remedy, to take off their clothes and lie down; that would have been too bold a step, not only for a young girl, but for a young goatherd also. And so night came again, bringing sleeplessness and recollection of what had been done and self-blame for what had been left undone. 'We kissed,' they thought, 'and it was no help. We embraced, and it did no good. Perhaps lying down

together is the only cure for Love. We must try that too; at least it'll be an improvement on kissing.'

10. After their minds had been occupied in this way, they naturally experienced dreams of desire, with kisses and embraces; and what they had refrained from by day, they did in their dreams, and lay naked together. Hence it came about that, on the following day, they rose from their beds more completely possessed by love than ever, and drove down their flocks with a rush in their hurry to be kissing, and ran forward with delighted smiles as soon as they saw each other. And sure enough they kissed, and the embrace followed; but the third remedy lagged behind, for Daphnis did not dare to mention it and Chloe did not care to initiate it—until by sheer chance they performed that act as well.

11. They were sitting together beneath the trunk of an oak; they had tasted the delights of kissing, and were gorging on that pleasure with an appetite that felt as if it could never be satisfied. There were embraces, too, that crushed their bodies as their lips came together. Then Daphnis drew Chloe to him in a particularly violent caress—she somehow rolled onto her side, and Daphnis, as he pressed home his kiss, ended up lying alongside her. Both knew that this was the very image of their dream, and they lay there for a long time as though held in bonds. But they had no idea of what comes next, and believed that the pleasure of love went no further than this. At length, after a day spent mostly in frustration, they withdrew from each other's arms and drove their flocks homewards, loathing the coming of night.

Even so, it is possible that they would soon have made love in earnest, if the whole countryside had not suddenly been plunged into turmoil for the following reason.

12. Some rich young men from Methymna* took a notion to pass the vintage-time in a pleasure-tour. They launched a yacht, put their slaves to the oars, and proceeded to sail parallel to the territory of the Mytilenaeans which lies next to the sea. They chose that coast because it has good harbours and is richly endowed with country villas, and there are numerous thermal establishments and sporting estates and forests, of which latter some are nature's work, and others owe their existence to human

good-taste. To be young amid such scenes was altogether heavenly. As they alternately coasted along and put into harbour, they
did no harm whatsoever, but indulged in a variety of pleasant
diversions: sometimes they sat on a rock projecting into the sea
and fished the crevices below, using hooks dangling by a thin
cord from bamboo canes, and sometimes they took dogs and nets
and caught hares fleeing from the commotion amongst the vines,
and sometimes they amused themselves by fowling, and caught
wild geese and duck and bustard in snares. And so their sport
kept their table supplied. If they needed anything extra, they got
it from the country-people, handing over more money than its
real value. But all that they required was bread and wine and
shelter—lodgings were necessary, because the season was now
late autumn, and it was unsafe to remain at sea all the time;
accordingly they always pulled their vessel on shore in case a
storm blew up during the night.

13. This proved to be their undoing; because one of the rustics, short of a rope for hauling up the great stone that squeezed
the trodden grapes a second time, the old rope having broken,
went unnoticed to the sea-shore, approached the vessel while it
was lying unguarded, untied the mooring-cable, took it home, and
used it for the aforesaid purpose. Next morning the young men
searched for their cable; when no one owned up to the theft, they
rebuked their hosts mildly, and then continued their voyage along
the coast. After covering thirty stades they came to land at the
fields where Daphnis and Chloe lived—they thought that the
plain would be a good place for hare-hunting. They did not have a
rope for mooring the ship, but twisted long, green withies into a
rope and by this means secured the ship to the land by its stern.
Then they let loose their dogs to cast round for a scent, and
spread their nets across the most promising paths. The dogs
dashed about barking and terrified the goats, who left the higher
ground and ran down closer to the sea. They could find nothing
to eat in the sand, however; and the upshot was that they wandered up to the ship, and the bolder ones devoured the green
withies that moored it to the shore.

14. Just then a wind began to blow from the mountains, and the sea became rougher. In a trice the undertow of the ebbing waves had caught the ship—which was already floating free—and was carrying it out to sea. The Methymnaeans saw what was happening, and some of them ran down to the strand, while others collected the dogs together. All were shouting, which alerted the people working in the nearby fields and brought them running to the shore. But there was nothing that anyone could do, because the breeze continued to freshen, and the ship was swept along by the current too fast to be caught.

Now, the young men had lost a good deal of property, and they naturally wanted to know who was in charge of the goats; on finding Daphnis, they pummelled him and stripped him of his clothes, and one of them went so far as to pick up a dog-leash and twist his hands behind his back with the intention of tying them. When Daphnis was struck he cried out and begged the country-folk to rescue him, appealing for help to Lamon and Dryas above all. These two held on to him resolutely—they were tough old fellows, hard-handed from their toil on the farm—and demanded that the dispute should be settled by arbitration.

15. Everyone approved of this suggestion, and so they appointed Philetas the cowherd to sit as judge—he was the oldest man present, and among the local people he had the reputation of being scrupulously just. First, the Methymnaeans made their accusation—they kept it clear and brief, because (thought they) the judge was only a cowherd.

'We came to these fields because we wanted to hunt. We tied up our ship with green withies, therefore, and left it beside the shore, while we ourselves took our dogs and set them to look for game. In the meantime the defendant's goats came down to the sea and ate the withy-rope, and cast the ship loose. You saw it adrift on the sea—can you imagine how full it is of our possessions? Think what we have lost in the way of clothes, and harness for our dogs, and money! One could have bought this whole estate with what was in that ship! In lieu of which we claim the right to arrest this man as an incompetent goatherd, because he pastures his goats at the seaside, as though he were a sailor.'

16. That was how the Methymnaeans put the case for the

prosecution. Now, Daphnis was in a poor state after his beating; but when he saw Chloe in the audience, he felt superior to them all, and made this speech:

'I pasture my goats in the proper way; not one person in this whole countryside has ever alleged that my goats have devoured any man's garden or broken the young shoots of his vines. But my accusers are incompetent hunters and their dogs are ill-trained; with their running about and their fierce barking they drove my goats from the hills and the plains to the sea. These dogs were more like wolves! "Your goats ate the withy-rope", say my accusers. Well, so they did, for they had no grass or arbutus or thyme on the sands. "The wind and the sea lost us the ship." But that was the doing of a squall, and not of the goats. "There were clothes and money on board." Now, who in their senses would believe that a ship carrying so much of value had withies for its mooring-rope?'

17. Daphnis burst into tears as he came to the end of his plea, and this moved the rustics to plentiful sympathy; Philetas the judge swore by Pan and the Nymphs that Daphnis was not guilty of any wrongful act, and no more were his goats, but the guilty parties were the sea and the wind, and it was for other powers to pass judgement on *them*. But Philetas failed to convince the Methymnaeans when he put his verdict to them—instead, they pushed forward angrily, trying to seize Daphnis again, and made as if to tie his hands together. This alarmed the country-folk, who descended on them like a cloud of starlings or jackdaws;* they quickly pulled Daphnis free—he was already hitting out lustily on his own behalf—and just as quickly put the Methymnaeans to flight with blows of their cudgels. Nor did they leave off until they had driven them past their own borders and into another district.

18. While the others were pursuing the Methymnaeans, Chloe led Daphnis very gently to the Nymphs' grotto; she washed his face, which was bloodstained from a cut on his nose where a punch had landed, and then took from her knapsack a piece of leavened bread and a segment of cheese, which she made him eat. But what did most to restore him was the kiss she gave him, making her lips delectably soft, a honey-sweet kiss.

19. So Daphnis had another narrow escape. That was not how the affair ended, however. The Methymnaeans had a miserable journey home—they had been reduced from yachtsmen to tramps, from overfed playboys to walking wounded—and on their arrival they called an assembly of the citizens and presented a petition begging for revenge. Of what had really happened they told not a word, since they were afraid that, over and above everything else, they would be ridiculed for allowing themselves to be so humiliated by shepherds. Instead, they accused the Mytilenaeans of taking away their ship and seizing their possessions by an act of war. The citizens were easily led to believe them because of their wounds, and as the young men belonged to the foremost families in the state, they thought it only right to take vengeance on their behalf; so they voted to attack the Mytilenaeans without sending any herald to declare war, and issued orders to their general to launch ten warships and pillage the enemy coast—it was dangerous to risk a larger fleet at sea, with winter so close at hand.

20. Next day the general lost no time in putting to sea, and, with his soldiers at the oars, sailed against the Mytilenaean farmlands on the coast. He carried off many herds and flocks, seized large quantities of corn and wine—the vintage having ended not long before—and took prisoner a considerable number of the workpeople. In the course of his operations he raided the country where Chloe and Daphnis had their homes, making a lightning descent and driving away as booty all the livestock that came in his path. Daphnis was not herding his goats, but had gone up into the wood and was cutting green, leafy branches so that he would have fodder to give the kids in the winter. When the attack took place, therefore, he saw it from above and promptly hid himself in the hollow trunk of a dead beech-tree. But Chloe was with the sheep and goats—she was pursued, and fled for sanctuary to the Nymphs' grotto, where she begged the raiders to spare her and her charges for the goddesses' sake. It was no use; the Methymnaeans heaped insults on the holy images, then drove away the animals and made Chloe their captive—they beat her as though she were a goat or a sheep, using withies for whips.

21. Their ships were now full of plunder of every sort, and so they decided not to go any further, but set out on the homeward voyage, being equally afraid of their enemies and of the winter. The Methymnaeans, then, sailed away; they had to toil at their oars, because there was no wind. When all was quiet again Daphnis went down to the plain where he and Chloe kept their flocks. No goats did he see, no sheep could he find, no Chloe did he encounter, but what met him was a great emptiness—and, lying where they had been dropped, the pan-pipes that Chloe loved to play. He uttered loud cries and piteous wails; he ran in turn to the oak-tree where they always sat, and to the shore, hoping to find her there, and to the Nymphs, with whom Chloe had sought refuge when pursued. Going into the cave, he flung himself to the ground and started to reproach the Nymphs and accuse them of betrayal.

22. 'Was Chloe torn from you,' he said, 'while you stood idly by?—Chloe, who always wove you the garlands that you wear, and poured you a share of the first of the milk, and dedicated her pan-pipes to you—see, there they hang! Not one goat have the wolves ever taken from me, but these enemies have stolen my whole herd and the girl who kept her sheep beside me, and now they will skin the hide off the goats and make sacrifices of the sheep, and Chloe will have to spend the rest of her life in a city. How can I go slinking home to my father and mother without my goats and without Chloe, with a workless future staring me in the face? For I have nothing to pasture now. All I can do is lie here and wait for death or another war. Oh Chloe, are your sufferings as bad as mine? Do you remember this plain and the Nymphs here, and me? The sheep and goats are prisoners with you—do they give you any comfort?'

23. His tears and sorrow gave way to a deep sleep, which overtook him even as he was speaking. And while he slept the three Nymphs appeared to him in all their comeliness and lofty stature, bare-armed and sandal-less, with hair unbound, and like their statues. At first they seemed to be pitying Daphnis; but presently the eldest spoke to him with words of good cheer:

'Spare us your reproaches, Daphnis, because our care for Chloe outdoes yours. In her infancy, too, we took pity on her and nursed her when she lay abandoned in this cave. Now likewise have we taken thought for her well-being, lest she be carried to Methymna and made a slave, or be numbered among the common spoils of war. And so did we entreat Pan to be Chloe's rescuer—Pan yonder, who has his statue beneath the pine-tree, the god whom you and Chloe have never honoured,* even with a flower or two—for he knows more of army-camps than we, and many a time before today has he left his country solitude and gone to war; and when he marches against the Methymnaeans they will find him an evil enemy! Be not troubled, therefore, but arise and show yourself to Lamon and Myrtale, who are lying like you upon the ground, because they think that you are made prisoner with the other booty. For Chloe will return to you tomorrow, with the goats and with the sheep, and you two will graze your flocks together and play your pipes together. All else concerning you and Chloe will be for Love to accomplish.'

24. Daphnis jumped up out of sleep full of what he had seen and heard; sobbing with joy and sorrow, he prostrated himself before the Nymphs' statues, and made a vow to sacrifice the best of his she-goats if Chloe should be saved. He also ran to the pine-tree where the image of Pan stood, goat-legged and horned, with pipes in one hand and a leaping billy-goat in the other; he saluted Pan with the same act of reverence, and prayed for Chloe and promised to sacrifice a billy-goat. At last, when it was almost sunset, he stopped weeping and praying, shouldered the branches that he had cut, and went back to the cottage, where he set Lamon and the others free from their grief and filled them with joy; then he had something to eat, and without more ado lay down to sleep—though not a tearless sleep, what with his prayers that he would dream of the Nymphs again and day would quickly come, the day on which they had promised him Chloe. That was the longest night that Daphnis had ever known. And here is what happened during these hours.

25. After sailing about ten stades on the way home, the Methymnaean general wanted to give some respite to his soldiers, who were tired out with the labour of raiding. Ahead of him there

loomed a promontory that planted its feet in the deep water and
then prolonged itself in the shape of a crescent, inside which the
sea made a calmer haven than any harbour. When he had rounded
this cape, therefore, the general stationed his ships at anchor well
off shore, so that none was vulnerable to attack from the land by
peasants. Then he gave his Methymnaeans leave to enjoy themselves as though they were at peace. Their plunder provided them
with plenty of everything, and so they drank and frolicked and
gave a good imitation of a holiday held to celebrate some great
victory.

Day was just ending, and the approach of night was bringing
their jamboree to a close, when suddenly all the land seemed to
glow with fire, and a rushing noise of oars was heard, as if a big
fleet were sailing to attack them. One of the Methymnaeans
yelled out an order to arm, another summoned the general; one
man seemed to have been wounded, and one was lying flat on the
ground in a corpse-like attitude. To all intents and purposes a
night-attack was going on, but no enemies were there.

26. What befell them in the night was bad enough; but the day
that followed was still more frightening. Ivy and ivy-berries
appeared on the horns of Daphnis' billy-goats and nanny-goats,
while Chloe's rams and ewes gave forth blood-curdling wolf-
howls. Chloe herself was seen to be wearing a crown of pine-
sprigs. The sea, too, became a place of marvels; the anchors
stayed at the bottom when the crews tried to raise them, the oars
shattered when they lowered them to begin rowing, and dolphins
leapt out of the sea and thumped the ships with their tails until
the timbers were loosened. A warbling of pan-pipes was heard at
the top of the cliff which dropped sheer from under the headland
into the sea; it did not delight the listeners as pipes should, however, but terrified them like a trumpet-blast. And so they were
overcome with panic and flew to arms and gave a phantom army
the name of enemies. All this made them pray for night to come
back, because they hoped to be granted a truce after dark. These
happenings were no mystery, of course, to all discerning people,
who knew that the source of the sounds and apparitions was Pan's
resentment at something that the sailors had done; they, however,

were unable to make out the cause—they had not taken plunder
from any holy place of Pan—until, about noon, the general fell
into a supernatural sleep, and Pan appeared to him in person, and
spoke as follows:

27. 'O men who exceed all others in ungodliness and impiety,
what madness has driven you to venture on these brazen
deeds?*—You have filled with war the countryside that I love,
you have stolen the herds of cattle and goats and sheep that are
my care, you have dragged from the altars a girl whom Love
desires to make into a myth, and have felt no shame before the
Nymphs, who witnessed your sacrilege, or before me, Pan. Never,
therefore, will you see Methymna, if you sail onwards with your
ill-gotten booty, nor will you escape these pipes of mine that have
driven you to distraction, but I will sink you to the bottom of the
sea and make you food for the fishes—unless you make haste to
return Chloe to the Nymphs and her animals to Chloe, both goats
and sheep. Rise, then, and set on land the girl and all the other
things that I say, and I will guide you on your voyage and her on
her road.'

28. This dream unnerved Bryaxis—that was the general's
name—and he leapt up, summoned the captains of his ships, and
ordered an immediate search to be made among the prisoners for
Chloe. She was soon found and brought before him, for she was
sitting with the pine-crown on her head. Bryaxis thought that this
tallied with his dream-vision, and accordingly he conveyed Chloe
to the land on his own flagship. She was no sooner ashore than the
sound of pan-pipes was heard again from the cliff—now, though,
it was no longer warlike and intimidating, but resembled the
piping of a shepherd, which leads the flocks to pasture; and the
sheep went hurrying out of the ship and down the gangway,
slipping and sliding on the cleats of their hooves, while the goats
stepped far more boldly, because they were used to walking down
precipices.

29. And then they all gathered in a circle round Chloe, just
like dancers in a reel, skipping and bleating and giving every sign
of joy; but the goats belonging to the other goatherds stayed
where they were in the ship's hold, as though the music had no

power over them, and so did the sheep and cattle. Everyone was amazed, and they began to salute Pan with cries of good omen. But even as they did so, still greater miracles were seen in both elements, on the land and in the sea: the Methymnaean ships began to move off before their crews could pull up the anchors, and a leaping dolphin guided the general's ship on its way; and meanwhile a ravishing sound of pan-pipes led the goats and sheep—though no one could see the piper. And so sheep and goats meandered along, feeding as they went, their ears caressed by the melody.

30. It was about the hour of the second grazing when Daphnis looked out from a high vantage-point and saw the flocks and Chloe. He gave a great cry of 'Oh Nymphs and Pan!' then darted down to the plain and flung his arms round Chloe—after which he fell down in a swoon. But Chloe kissed him and held him tenderly in her embrace until he slowly came to himself again; and then he went to the old, familiar oak-tree, and sat down under its trunk, and asked her how she had got away from the enemy when there were so many of them. Chloe answered by telling him her story in full: the ivy on the goats' horns, the howling of the sheep, the pine that had sprung forth on her head, the fire on the land and the noises on the sea, the pan-pipes with their two tunes, one warlike and the other peaceful, the night of terror, and how, when she did not know the way, music had shown her the way. In all this Daphnis recognized his dream of the Nymphs and the agency of Pan; and he in his turn told Chloe what he had seen and heard—he would have died, he confessed, had not the Nymphs given him reason to live. Then he dispatched Chloe to bring Dryas and Lamon and their friends and, at the same time, all the things that are proper for a sacrifice. Meanwhile, he caught the finest of his she-goats, crowned it with a wreath of ivy—just as the goats had appeared to the enemy— poured milk over its horns, and sacrificed it to the Nymphs; then he hung it from the bough of a tree, skinned it, and made an offering of the hide.

31. By this time Chloe had arrived with her party. Daphnis lit a fire, on which he boiled some of the meat and roasted the rest;

he gave the first portion to the Nymphs, and then poured out a full mixing-bowl of new wine, as a drink-offering, and spread couches of leaves on the ground. After that he regaled the company with food and drink and merriment—while still keeping a watchful eye on the flocks in case a wolf got amongst them and dealt with them like an invading army. They sang, too, some songs in praise of the Nymphs, made up by shepherds long ago. When night came on they lay down to sleep where they were in the open. Next day they turned their thoughts to Pan; they took the billy-goat who was leader of the herd, garlanded him with pine, and led him to the pine-tree; then they poured an offering of wine and sacrificed him, acclaiming Pan as they did so; then they hung up the carcass, removed the hide, roasted or boiled the meat, and put it down on the leafy couches, close at hand in the meadow; as for the hide, they nailed it up, horns and all, on the pine-tree beside the statue of Pan—a shepherds' offering to a shepherds' god. They served Pan from the meat, they poured him wine from a bigger bowl. Chloe sang and Daphnis piped.

32. After these ceremonies they all reclined on the couches and were busy eating when, by pure chance, along came Philetas the cowherd, bringing Pan some garlands and some bunches of grapes, attached to their branches and complete with leaves; he was accompanied by his youngest son, Tityrus, an auburn-haired and grey-eyed boy, with white skin and a haughty look and a step as light and frisky as a kid's. The banqueters jumped to their feet and helped to garland Pan and tie the vine-branches to the foliage of the pine-tree; then they made Philetas lie down next to them and treated him as one of the party. Old men that they were, when they began to be a little drunk they gossiped together about many things: how they had been herdsmen when they were young, and how they had survived many a pirate-raid; one claimed credit for killing a wolf, another for being second only to Pan at piping—this last was the boast of Philetas,

33. and it made Daphnis and Chloe try with all their might to persuade him to give them a sample of his skill and play his pipes at the feast of a god who delights in piping. Philetas said that he would—although complaining that old age had spoiled his

wind—and took Daphnis' pan-pipes. But these pipes were too small for Philetas' great technique, because they were intended for blowing by a boy's mouth. So Philetas sent Tityrus for his own pipes, his cottage being ten stades away. Tityrus flung aside his over-garment and set off running with naked limbs, moving as gracefully as a fawn. While they waited for him to return, Lamon undertook to tell them the legend of how pan-pipes were invented: a Sicilian goatherd had sung him this tale, and it had cost Lamon a billy-goat and a set of pipes.

34. 'Long ago,' he began, 'these pan-pipes were not a musical instrument but a beautiful girl with a tuneful voice. She herded goats, joined the Nymphs in their play, and sang as she sings today. While she herded and played and sang, Pan came and tried to persuade her to do his will—he promised to give all her nanny-goats twin kids, if she would be his. But the girl mocked his love, and said that she would not have for her lover a creature who was not fully goat or man. Pan made to pursue her and take her by brute-force; but Syrinx ran away from him and his brute-force.

> Fleeing,
> fainting,
> she hid in the reeds,
> she sank into the swamp.
> Pan slashed the reeds in wrath,
> but found the maiden not,
> and knew her end.

And thus he invented the musical instrument, when he stuck the reeds together with wax, making their lengths unequal, because love, too, had proved, for him and her, a thing unequal. And she who once was a maiden fair, is now the *Pipes of Pan*, and makes melody.'

35. Lamon had just come to the end of his story, and Philetas was complimenting him on telling a tale more honeyed than song, when Tityrus came back with the pipes for his father—they were a big instrument, with individual pipes of great size, and the wax between them was decorated with bronze; you could have imagined that they were the very pipes that Pan first made.

Philetas rose from his couch of leaves and went to where he could sit upright. He first tested the pipes to see whether they were giving the air free passage; then, finding that his breath was passing through them without hindrance, he started to blow *fortissimo*—it was like listening to a whole pipe-band, so loudly did the blast resound! Little by little, though, he blew with less force and altered the tune to a sweeter note; and then, demonstrating the whole art of orderly pasturing to the sound of music, he piped successively in the style that is proper for a herd of oxen, the one that suits a herd of goats, and the one that pleases sheep. The sheep-music was sweet, the ox-music was ample, the goat-music was shrill. I can best describe his playing if I say that he made one set of pan-pipes sound like all the pan-pipes in the world.

36. While the others lay without a sound, transported with pleasure, Dryas stood up and told Philetas to play a Dionysiac melody. Then he gave them the vintage-dance, miming all the different stages—now he was gathering the grapes, now he carried baskets; next he trod the grapes, and then he filled the jars, and then he drank the new wine. Dryas danced all these actions in so graceful and lifelike a way that they seemed to see the vines and the wine-press and the jars and Dryas really drinking.

37. So Dryas, with his dancing, became the third old man to put up a good show, and at the end of his performance he kissed Chloe and Daphnis. They instantly rose and danced the story that Lamon had told, Daphnis taking the part of Pan, and Chloe playing Syrinx. He implored and cajoled, she smiled and disdained; he pursued her, running on tip-toe to imitate Pan's hooves, she portrayed the girl wilting in her flight. Then Chloe ran to the wood and hid, as though she were vanishing into the swamp, while Daphnis picked up the great pipes of Philetas and blew a strain that moped, as if he sickened for love; was amorous, as if he would persuade; and cried 'Return to me!' as if he searched. Philetas was amazed—he jumped up, kissed Daphnis, and followed the kiss by presenting him with the pipes; then he prayed that Daphnis would bequeath them in his turn to as worthy a successor.

38. Daphnis dedicated his own pipes to Pan—such little pipes!—and then, after kissing Chloe as lovingly as though she had really run away and been found again, he drove his herd homewards, piping as he went, for it was now night. And Chloe likewise drove her flock homewards, calling them together by the music of her own pipes; and the goats ambled next to the sheep, and Daphnis walked beside Chloe. They engrossed each other's attention until it was quite dark, when they arranged to drive their animals down to the plain at an earlier hour on the following day.

And so they did, for day was just breaking when they came to the grazing-ground. After saluting the gods of the place—the Nymphs first, and then Pan—they sat down beneath the oak-tree and played their pipes; then they kissed each other, embraced, lay down together—and got up again without having done anything more. They saw to their dinner, and drank wine mixed with milk.

39. All these circumstances made them hotter and bolder, so that they began to wrangle with one another as lovers will, and gradually they advanced from that to making promises on oath. Daphnis strode over to the pine-tree and swore by Pan not to endure life without Chloe for even a single day, and Chloe went into the cave and swore by the Nymphs to be with Daphnis all her life, and to die when he died. But Chloe's youth and virginity made her so sincere that, as she left the cave, she resolved to bind Daphnis by a second oath.

'Daphnis,' said she, 'Pan is a lustful and faithless god. He loved Pitys, he loved Syrinx, and he never stops bothering the tree-nymphs and pestering the nymphs who protect the flocks. And so he'll neglect to punish you for neglect of your oaths to him, even if you go after more women than pan-pipes have reeds. I want you to swear to me by this herd of goats and by that she-goat who nursed you that you will never desert Chloe while she stays true to you. But if she wrongs you and the Nymphs, you must shun her and loathe her and kill her as you would a wolf.'

Daphnis was pleased with Chloe for her fond distrust; he went into the middle of the herd, and then, holding a nanny-goat with one hand and a billy-goat with the other, he swore to love Chloe

while she loved him, and, if she ever preferred another, to kill . . .
not her but himself. That made Chloe glad in turn, and she had
faith in Daphnis because she was young and a virgin, and because
she was a shepherdess and believed that the goats and sheep are
the shepherds' and goatherds' very own gods.

BOOK 3

1. When* the citizens of Mytilene heard about the attack of the ten ships, and reports of the plundering were brought to them by people arriving from the country, they had no mind to put up with such treatment from the Methymnaeans, but resolved to make an armed response without delay. They called up three thousand infantry and five hundred cavalry, and dispatched the general Hippasus with this force by the overland route, mistrusting the sea in winter.

2. While on the march, Hippasus scorned to pillage the fields of the Methymnaeans or carry off the herds and possessions of their farmers and shepherds, because he regarded that as the conduct of a brigand rather than a general; instead, he quickly made for the capital, hoping to carry the gates before a guard was placed on them. But while he was still about a hundred stades from the city, he was met by a herald who brought the offer of a truce—the Methymnaeans had learned from their prisoners that the townspeople of Mytilene knew nothing about the unfortunate incident, but that the culprits were farmers and shepherds, who had treated the young men as they did because the latter had tried to take the law into their own hands; the Methymnaeans now regretted having acted towards a neighbouring city with more energy than wisdom, and they were anxious to return all their booty and to resume friendly relations with Mytilene on land and sea without fear of reprisal. Hippasus sent the herald on to Mytilene, even though his commission was invested with full powers of negotiation; he himself pitched camp about ten stades short of Methymna and awaited orders from his city. After a two-day interval a messenger came with instructions to accept the return of the booty and return home without doing any damage—offered a choice between war and peace, they judged peace to be more advantageous.

3. Thus ended the war between Methymna and Mytilene, as unlooked for in its conclusion as in its onset. And now there came a winter that was more irksome to Daphnis and Chloe than the war had been. A sudden, heavy snowfall blocked all the roads and shut in all the peasants. Mountain-streams became raging torrents, and there was ice everywhere. The trees bent under the weight of snow until it seemed that their boughs would break; the whole earth disappeared from view except here and there at the margins of springs and streams. It was so bad that no one drove his flock to pasture or put his nose outside the door; instead, they made a good fire at cock-crow, and then spent the day spinning flax or combing out the hair of their goats or tying bird-snares. While the snow lasted, the livestock needed special care—the cattle were fed bran at their mangers, the goats and sheep leafy twigs in their folds, the pigs mast and acorns in their sties.

4. Now that all were kept at home willy-nilly, the other farmers and herdsmen congratulated themselves on getting a brief holiday from work and having time for a proper breakfast in the morning and a nice lie-in; they voted winter a better time than summer and autumn—more enjoyable, even, than the spring. Not so our two lovers! Remembering departed joys—their kisses and embraces and the delightful picnics which they had shared— they passed sleepless nights and doleful days, and waited for the spring, that rebirth after death. They felt wistful if there came into their hands some haversack which they had often taken their food from, or if they saw a milk-pail which they had often drunk from together, or, cast carelessly aside, pan-pipes once given as a token of love. And so they prayed to the Nymphs and Pan to rescue them from this new chapter of troubles and show them and their flocks the long-awaited sun; and, as well as praying, they tried to think of a plan for getting a sight of one another. Chloe was woefully short of ways and means of bringing this to pass, because her mother (as Chloe regarded her) was always at her side, teaching her how to card wool and keep the spindle turning, and ever and anon raising the subject of marriage. But Daphnis had time to spare, and he was more resourceful than a girl could be; consequently he invented a ploy for seeing Chloe. And here is what it was.

5. Just outside Dryas' farmyard, right up against the fence, grew two big myrtle-bushes and a swag of ivy, the myrtles standing quite close together and the ivy filling the space between them—it put out its runners, like a vine, to the myrtle on either side, and made a sort of cave by intertwining its foliage with theirs; clusters of berries hung from it, as abundant and large as bunches of grapes on the branches of a vine. The winter-birds came flocking round the ivy, because there was little for them to eat in the wild; there were throngs of blackbirds and crowds of thrushes, there were wood-pigeons and starlings and every other feathered creature that eats ivy-berries. Daphnis made the excuse that he was going out to catch these birds, and sallied forth; he had packed his knapsack with pieces of roasted meat spread with honey, and he was carrying birdlime and snares just like your genuine bird-catcher. Now, although Dryas' farm was not more than ten stades distant, the snow was lying as deep as ever, and it made Daphnis toil hard. But Love can go anywhere—

thorough flood, thorough fire

and Scythian snow!*

6. So Daphnis was positively running when he arrived outside Dryas' yard. He shook the snow from his legs, set the snares, and smeared the birdlime on some long twigs. Then he sat down and thought anxiously about birds and Chloe. About the birds he need not have worried—lots came, and enough were taken for him to be kept busy gathering them in, wringing their necks, and plucking their feathers. But no one came out from the farmyard, not man or woman, or even a hen; they were all shut fast inside, hugging the fire. Daphnis was in a quandary—those dratted birds, thought he, were birds of ill omen so far as seeing Chloe was concerned! He began to toy with the idea of pushing brazenly through the door on the strength of some excuse; the question was, what could he say that was most convincing?

'I've come for some hot coals.'

'Haven't you neighbours on your doorstep?'—

'Can you let me have some bread?'

'But your knapsack's full of food!'—

'We're short of wine.'

'Out of wine? But you've only just picked your grapes!'—

'Help! There's a wolf at my heels!!!'

'So where are its tracks, then?'—

'I came to catch birds.'

'Well, why not go home now you've caught them?'—

'I want to see Chloe.'

'Now* who tells this tale to the girl's parents, eh?'—

There was always a snag, whatever he thought of to say. 'Well,' he reflected at last, 'if I can't speak without making them suspicious, I'd better keep quiet. I'll see Chloe in the spring, since it looks as though I'm not fated to see her in the winter.' These were his thoughts, more or less, as, in glum silence, he picked up the birds he had caught and began to plod homewards. What happened next can only be accounted for by supposing that Love had taken pity on Daphnis.

7. Dryas and the farmhands were gathered round the table; the pieces of meat were being apportioned, the loaves set out, and the wine mixed in its bowl. One of the sheepdogs had been waiting for this moment—when he saw that nobody was looking, he seized a lump of meat and vanished with it through the door. Great was Dryas' disgust at this, because the meat was his share; he snatched up a big stick and set off in hot pursuit, exactly like another dog. The chase led him past the ivy-bower, and there he saw Daphnis, who had just shouldered the dead birds and decided to move off. Immediately Dryas forgot both dog and dinner; he gave a loud shout of 'Well met, lad!' and followed this by throwing his arms round Daphnis and kissing him heartily. Then, still keeping hold of Daphnis, he led him into the house. When Daphnis and Chloe set eyes on each other, it was all they could do not to faint! They just managed to stay upright and exchange greetings and kisses—it was clinging together that propped them up and stopped them from collapsing!

8. So Daphnis got two things that he had given up hoping for—Chloe and a kiss; he took a place at the fire, and swung the pigeons and blackbirds from his back onto the table. Then he told

them how he had gone out hunting because he was bored with
staying indoors, and how he had caught some of the birds with
snares and some with birdlime, when they were tempted by the
myrtle-berries and the ivy. Daphnis' energetic behaviour
impressed his hosts, and they told him to help himself from what
the dog had left. They also told Chloe to pour out drinks; whereupon she smilingly served the others, but left Daphnis to the
last—she was pretending to be cross with him for being ready to
go home without seeing her, after coming almost to her door. She
made it up to him, though, by taking a sip from his cup before
parting with it—only after that did she pass the cup to Daphnis;
and he drank the wine slowly, thirsty though he was, because by
taking his time he gave himself a longer-lasting pleasure.

9. Soon the table was clear of bread and meat, but they still sat
on. The farmer and his wife enquired after the health of Myrtale
and Lamon, and said how lucky these two were to be blessed with
such a son to take care of them in their old age. Daphnis positively glowed at being praised in Chloe's hearing; and when they
asked him to stay the night because they were going to sacrifice to
Dionysus next day, he was so over-the-moon that he nearly kissed
their feet instead of the god's! Next minute he seized his knapsack and emptied out a good share of his meat-and-honey snacks,
plus all the birds that he had caught—these they started to prepare for the evening meal. A second bowl of wine was put down
and a second fire set blazing; in no time at all it was dark, and they
were devouring their second dinner of the day. Afterwards, they
told stories and sang ballads. Then it was time for bed, Chloe
sleeping with her mother and Dryas with Daphnis. Chloe had
nothing to comfort her but the prospect of seeing Daphnis in the
morning. Daphnis, on the other hand, found a pleasure to indulge
in, though of a sadly fruitless kind: he thought it delightful to
share a bed even with Chloe's father, with the result that he spent
the night pawing and kissing Dryas—the silly boy was doing it all
to Chloe in his dreams!

10. When morning came, the cold was beyond belief, and a
breeze from the north was drying everything to tinder. But they
turned out nevertheless, and sacrificed a ram lamb* to Dionysus,

after which they made a roaring fire and began preparations for the feast. Since Nape was baking bread and Dryas was boiling the ram, Daphnis and Chloe were left without anything to do; and they took the chance to go out of the farmyard to the ivy-bower, where they once more set snares and put lime on twigs, and took another good haul of birds. They also found time for a perfect orgy of kissing and some exquisitely enjoyable talk:

'I came because of *you*, Chloe.'

'I know, Daphnis.'—

'It's for your sake that I've been murdering the wretched blackbirds.'

'How can I show you how much I care?'—

'Just remember me!'

'Oh but I do remember you, by the Nymphs! I swore by them that day in the cave—and we'll go there again as soon as the snow melts.'—

'But the snow's deep, Chloe. I'm afraid I'll melt before it!'

'Don't be downhearted, Daphnis—the sun's hot.'—

'I wish it were as hot as the fire that's burning my heart!'

'You're only joking—you don't mean it.'—

'I'm not joking—I swear it by the goats that you made *me* swear by!'

11. Daphnis had only to speak, and Chloe would answer him like an echo. Their dialogue went on until Nape's helpers came calling them to table; whereupon they ran indoors, weighed down with far more birds than Daphnis had caught the day before. They took some wine from the mixing-bowl and poured it as an offering to Dionysus; then they put ivy-garlands on their heads, and ate the sacrificial meal. When the time came for Daphnis to go home, they sent him on his way with Bacchic cries of 'Iacche!' and 'Euai!' They had filled his knapsack with loaves and meat, and had also given him the pigeons and thrushes to take to Lamon and Myrtale, because they knew that they could catch others for themselves so long as winter lasted and the ivy did not fail. In taking his leave, Daphnis kissed Dryas and Nape before Chloe—he wanted to keep her kiss unspoiled on his lips.

And that day was not the end of it; he invented many more

schemes for making many more journeys in Chloe's direction—
and so they were not completely starved of love, despite the
winter.

12. And now it was the beginning of spring: the snow thawed,
the earth was laid bare, and the new grass peeped forth. The
herdsmen drove their animals out to pasture, and before them all
went Daphnis and Chloe, because *they* were servants of a Greater
Shepherd. Straightaway they sped to the Nymphs and the cave,
then to Pan and the pine-tree, and after that to the oak, under
which they sat down and watched their flocks, and kissed and
caressed each other fondly. Afterwards, wishing to make garlands
for the gods, they went to look for wild flowers; these were just
being coaxed from the ground by the fostering breath of the west
wind and the warming rays of the sun, but they succeeded in
finding violets and narcissi and pimpernels and other tributes
that earliest spring is wont to bear. They also took new milk from
some of the nanny-goats and ewes, and poured the Nymphs a
drink of it when they garlanded their statues. They made another
kind of offering by playing their pipes, as though trying to pro-
voke the nightingales to begin their music—whereupon those
singers sounded faintly from deep within the thickets, and little
by little and ever more clearly framed the name of Itys,* as if
remembering their song after the long winter's silence.

13. On all sides the flock bleated and the lambs skipped joy-
ously before kneeling down to suck their mothers' teats. Meanwhile the rams were galloping after those ewes which had not yet
been mothers—they would straddle them and tup them, choos-
ing a different partner every time. Among the billy-goats, too,
there was pursuing and amorous mounting of the she-goats—
they even fought over them, and each one had his own harem and
took care not to let it be invaded when his back was turned.
Scenes like these would have made even old men feel frisky; and
our two adolescents, who were in the heyday of their blood and
had long been looking for a way to consummate their love, kin-
dled at the sounds and melted at the sights and tried to think how
they, too, could do something better than kissing and embracing.
Daphnis, in particular, was beset by these thoughts; charged as he

was with animal spirits after his confinement indoors and his enforced idleness during the winter, the kissing made him feel wanton and the embracing made him feel lascivious and he was meddlesome and impudent enough for any devilry.

14. And so he asked Chloe to grant him everything he wanted and lie naked with him for a longer time than they had done before—for, said Daphnis, of Philetas' instructions for administering the only cure for love, they had tried everything else but this. Chloe wanted to know what else there could be besides kissing and embracing and simply lying down, and what he intended to do after they were both naked and he had lain down with her.

'What the rams do to the ewes and the he-goats to the she-goats', said Daphnis. 'Don't you see how, after they've done what they do, the females don't run away from the males any more and the males don't weary themselves going after them, but from that time on they graze side-by-side as though they had enjoyed some kind of pleasure together? So what they do must be something sweet, that puts away the bitterness of love.'

'That's all very well, Daphnis,' quoth Chloe, 'but don't *you* see that the she-goats and the he-goats and the rams and the ewes do what they do with the males standing up, while the females stand up and let them do it—the males jumping up and the females making a back for them? Whereas you're expecting me to *lie down* with you and take my clothes off into the bargain, even though the ewes' coats are a lot thicker than my clothes are when I have them on!'

Daphnis gave in, and lay down with Chloe; for a long time he lay there without having the slightest idea how to do any of the things that he longed for so passionately. And so he made Chloe stand up again, and clung to her from behind in imitation of the billy-goats. But that only made him feel more baffled than ever; so he sat down and wept, to think that even the rams knew more about the deeds of love than he did.

15. Now Daphnis had a neighbour who farmed his own land, by name Chromis.* This man's youth was far behind him, but he cohabited with a woman from the town—she was young and pretty and too delicate for her rustic surroundings, and her name was Lycaenion.* She saw Daphnis daily, when he drove his goats past her house in the morning on their way to graze and when he returned with them in the evening, and she took a fancy to make him her lover, by enticing him with gifts. Following this plan, she waylaid him once when he was alone and gave him pan-pipes and a honeycomb and a knapsack made of doeskin; but she hesitated to speak, because she had guessed that he was in love with Chloe, from observing how enamoured he was of the girl's company. Their lively glances and their laughter told her to begin with. Then, early one morning, she told Chromis* that she was going to visit a neighbour whose baby was due, but instead shadowed Daphnis and Chloe and hid in the bushes to avoid being seen— she heard all that they said, and saw all that they did, and was looking on when Daphnis burst into tears. Lycaenion was touched by their obvious unhappiness, and at the same time she knew that she had been presented with a double opportunity— she could be the means of salvation to them, while getting what she dearly wanted for herself. So she went to work in the following way.

16. Next morning she left the house under the pretence of paying another visit to the expectant mother, went quite openly to the oak-tree where Daphnis and Chloe were sitting, and gave an accomplished performance in the role of a woman distraught.

'Oh Daphnis,' she cried, 'whatever shall I do? Help me, please help me, Daphnis! You know my twenty geese*—well, the pick of them has been carried off by an eagle! Its weight was too much for him, though, and he couldn't carry if aloft to his eyrie on that high crag, but fell with it into the forest down here. So I beg you by the Nymphs and by Pan yonder, come into the woods with me—because I daren't go alone—and save my goose! You mustn't let me be minus a bird! And maybe you'll kill the eagle too, and stop him stealing all those lambs and kids you keep on losing! Chloe will watch your herd meantime . . . I'm sure the goats all know her, because she's always so thick with you in the pasture.'

17. Little suspecting what was in store for him, Daphnis jumped up without hesitation, took his crook, and followed

Lycaenion's retreating figure. She led him as far from Chloe as she could; and when they came to the heart of the wood she made him sit down beside a spring and said:

'Listen, Daphnis: I know you're in love with Chloe—I heard all about it from the Nymphs, last night in a dream. They told me how you wept yesterday, and they've given me my orders—I'm to save you by teaching you the deeds of love. But the deeds I mean are not kissing and embracing and behaving like rams and billy-goats: they're another kind of leaping altogether, and it's a much nicer kind than what goes on in the herds, because you feel the pleasure for a longer time. So if you want to banish the blues and sample the delights you've set your heart on, all you have to do is make yourself my pupil, and I'll give you a lesson, as a favour to the Nymphs, our neighbours.'

18. Now Daphnis was only a country boy, just a humble goat-herd, and he was young and in love; and when he heard what Lycaenion was proposing, his joy knew no bounds—he flung himself down at her feet and begged her to teach him there and then the art of doing to Chloe the thing he wanted. And, as though he were on the point of receiving some great and truly god-sent teaching, he promised to give her a stall-fed kid and some soft cheeses made from the first squirts of milk from a she-goat, plus the goat herself. 'That's a bonus!' thought Lycaenion, who had never expected a goatherd to be so affluent. And then she began to teach Daphnis, like this:

She told him not to stand on ceremony, but to sit down beside her and kiss her as he usually kissed Chloe and just as often—and when he was in the middle of kissing he was to put his arms round her and lie down on the ground as he did so. After Daphnis had sat by her, kissed her, and lain down with her in his arms, Lycaenion could tell that he was able for love-making and all athrob with desire; so she made him raise himself a little from where he lay on his side, slid her body expertly under his, and guided him into the road which had eluded him till then. After that she didn't bother to do anything exotic—there was no need, because Nature herself taught him how to complete the act.

19. As soon as the lesson in love was over, Daphnis—who was

still a shepherd-boy at heart—wanted to run hot-foot to Chloe and do what he had been taught without a moment's delay, as though he were afraid that he might forget it if he lingered. But Lycaenion kept him back, and spoke again:

'You still have something to learn, Daphnis. I felt no pain this time round, because I'm a woman, not a girl—another man taught me this lesson long ago, and took my maidenhead as his recompense. But when Chloe struggles with you in this wrestling-match, she'll wail and weep and lie in a pool of blood. You mustn't fear the blood, though; but when she has agreed to let you have your way with her, bring her here, so that if she cries out, no one will hear, and if she weeps, no one will see, and if she bleeds, she can wash in the spring. And always remember that I made you a man before Chloe did!'

20. After Lycaenion had delivered this advice, she went away to another part of the wood as if she were still searching for her goose. Daphnis was left to digest her words; and as he turned them over in his mind, his eagerness abated, and he began to feel qualms about troubling Chloe for anything more intimate than kisses and embraces—the last thing that he wanted was to make her cry out as though at an enemy or weep as though in pain or bleed as though struck dead. For, being a novice in these matters, he shied away from the thought of blood, and believed (wrongly) that blood can only come from a wound. Resolved, therefore, to enjoy himself with Chloe in their old way, he stepped out of the wood and went to where she sat plaiting a garland of violets. He told her a white lie, by pretending that he had snatched the goose from the eagle's talons; and then he put his arms round her and kissed her as he had kissed Lycaenion in his moments of bliss— that was allowed, because there was no danger in it. Chloe responded by placing the garland carefully on his head and kissing his hair, which seemed to her more beautiful than the violets; then she took from her knapsack a wedge of preserved fruit and some small loaves, and gave Daphnis his dinner; and as he chewed, she stole morsels from his mouth, feeding exactly as if she were a baby-bird in the nest.

21. They were still eating—and busier kissing than eating—

when they saw a fishing-boat come sailing by. Wind was there none, but all was calm, so rowing was called for, and row the sailors did with might and main, for they were in haste to get their catch to Mytilene while it was fresh, to grace a rich man's table. As they swung forward over their oars, they did what seamen often do to beguile the toil of rowing—one man would be their boatswain* and sing them shanties, while the rest would take up the song in unison, like a choir, keeping time with his voice. So long as they were doing this on the open sea, their singing quickly died on the ear, as the sound faded into the airy spaces all round them; but when they had passed under a headland and run into a deeply curving bay, the rowers' voices could be heard more loudly, and the songs of the boatswains came clearly to the shore. For in the hills behind the level pasture there was a hollow coomb which received the sounds within itself, like a musical instrument, and then gave out a voice that mimicked every single thing that broke the silence—the noise of the oars, and the singing of the sailors, both separate, both distinct. And a pleasant thing it was to hear: first would come the voices from the sea, and afterwards, lagging as far behind in finishing as in starting, the voices from the land.

22. Now, Daphnis was no stranger to this phenomenon, and so he kept his attention entirely on the sea, relishing the spectacle as the boat skimmed past the shore quicker than a bird on the wing; he also tried to catch and memorize some of the songs, to add them to his piping repertoire. But Chloe was hearing an 'echo', as we call it, for the first time—she would look intently out to sea while the boatswains were trolling out the shanty, and then would turn and face the forest, as she tried to make out where the answering choir might be. When the sailors had gone rowing on their way and the coomb, too, was quiet again, Chloe asked Daphnis if there was not sea behind the headland as well, with another ship sailing by and other sailors singing the same tunes and silence falling on both companies at the same time. Daphnis found this question irresistibly amusing; but the laugh he gave was not more sweet than the kiss he pressed on Chloe's lips. And then, transferring the garland of violets from his head to hers, he

began to tell her the story of how the echo came into being; first, though, he made her promise him another ten kisses as his reward for teaching her.

23. 'You must know, my dear,' said he, 'that there are many kinds of nymphs—ash-tree nymphs, called Meliae, oak-tree nymphs, called Dryades, and nymphs of the marshes, called Heleioi. All are fair, all are makers of music. Echo was born the daughter of one of these—she was mortal because her father was mortal, and fair because her mother was fair. The nymphs reared her, and the Muses taught her to play the pan-pipes and the flute, to sing to the lyre and the cithara—in short, the whole of song. And so, when she grew to the full flower of her girlhood, she danced with the nymphs, and sang with the Muses. But male-kind did she altogether shun, both men and gods, because she loved virginity. Now Pan grew angry with this girl, from envy of her music, from hopeless longing for her beauty; he drove the shepherds and the goatherds mad, and they, like dogs or wolves, tore her in pieces, and cast her limbs—still singing—through all the world. In kindness to the nymphs, Earth hid these shreds of flesh and song, forgetting none, and gave their music shelter; and by the Muses' will do they send forth a voice and portray all things—gods, men, instruments, and beasts—as did that girl in olden time. Even Pan himself they mimic when he pipes, and, at the sound, up he jumps and gives pursuit across the mountains, with no desire in mind save this, to know who is his unseen pupil.'

When Daphnis ended his story, Chloe gave him not ten but ten-score kisses—for the echo had all but repeated what he said, as though to witness that he told no lie.

24. The sun was growing hotter every day, as the end of spring passed into the beginning of summer, and it was time again for new amusements, suitable for the summer days. Daphnis swam in the rivers, Chloe bathed in the springs. Daphnis piped in rivalry with the pine-trees, Chloe sang as if she wanted to outdo the nightingales. They hunted the chattering crickets, and caught the chirping cicadas. They gathered wild flowers, shook the fruit-trees, and ate the fruit. A time came, now, when they did after all lie down naked together, with one goatskin covering them both; and Chloe could easily have been made a woman, except that Daphnis was alarmed by the thought of blood. He actually forbade Chloe to go naked so often, because he was afraid that his resolution would give way in the end. Chloe was nonplussed at this, but she was too shy to ask the reason.

25. During this summer there was a throng of suitors round Chloe; they came from all over and presented themselves one after another at Dryas' cottage, asking for Chloe as their bride. Some brought a gift in their hands, others promised him a rich reward if they were the lucky candidate. Now Nape, for her part, was quite carried away by her hopes; she was all for betrothing Chloe, and against keeping at home any longer a girl of her age, who might lose her virginity any day in the pasture, and make a man of some shepherd just because he had given her a few apples or a bunch of roses; they ought, said Nape, to make Chloe mistress of her own house, while themselves accepting what was so generously offered and keeping it as a nest-egg for their own lawful son—because a male child had been born to them not long before. At times Dryas was impressed by her arguments, for every suitor was talking in terms of gifts far above the value of a shepherd-girl; but at other moments he reflected that the girl was too good for the farmers who were wooing her, and that, if she ever found her true parents, she would make him and his wealthy indeed. And so he put off replying, asked for more time, and then for still more, and meanwhile watched his harvest of gifts accumulating.

When Chloe heard of these developments her whole existence was darkened, and for quite a while she avoided Daphnis, because she did not want to grieve him. But when he refused to be put off and kept on demanding to know what was the matter, and was obviously suffering more by being kept in ignorance than he would have if he had known how matters stood, she told him all—how she had a host of rich suitors, what Nape was saying by way of forwarding her marriage, and how Dryas had not set his face against it, but had postponed it until the vintage-time.

26. These tidings knocked Daphnis all of a heap—he just sat

and cried his eyes out. Between his sobs, he could be heard exclaiming that he would die if Chloe deserted the pasture, and not only he, but her sheep, too, if their darling shepherdess were taken away. Soon, though, he pulled himself together and began to look on the bright side; he thought that he could win over Dryas, saw himself as one of Chloe's recognized wooers, and fancied his chances against the others. But one thing still worried him—Lamon's poverty; and that stopped him from nourishing any great hopes. Nevertheless, he was determined to enter the field, and Chloe seconded him. He did not dare to say a word to Lamon, but, plucking up his courage, he confessed his love to Myrtale, and discussed with her his prospects of marrying Chloe. Myrtale duly imparted this to her husband the same night. Her intercession fell on stony ground, however, and Lamon scoffed at her for proposing a match between the insignificant daughter of a shepherd-family and a youth who, judging by his birth-tokens, could look forward to high fortune, and who, if he were to find his own kin, would surely give his foster-parents their freedom and make them masters of a bigger farm. Knowing how deeply in love Daphnis was, Myrtale feared that he might be driven to some fatal act if all hope of marrying Chloe were denied him; and so she gave him a different version of Lamon's objections to the marriage.

'We're poor folk, my son, and we've more need of a bride for you who'll bring something with her. *They* are rich, and they'll be looking for a rich bridegroom.* But I'll tell you what you can do—get Chloe to persuade her father to give her leave to marry without asking a big price. No doubt she's as much in love with you as you are with her, and she'd rather go to bed with a handsome poor man than a well-off monkey.'

27. Myrtale thought that this was a harmless way of ensuring that the marriage would not take place, because she never expected Dryas to fall in with such a request when he had richer suitors to choose from. Daphnis could not fault her advice, but he knew that far more was being asked than he would ever be able to pay. So he did what penniless lovers have always done—he wept, and once more begged the Nymphs to come to his rescue. They came that very night while he slept, and everything about them was the same as when they had appeared to him before. As then, it was the eldest who spoke.

'Chloe's marriage', she said, 'is another god's concern. But *we* will give you gifts that will disarm Dryas. The yacht belonging to the Methymnaean youths, whereof your goats once ate the withy-rope, was carried by the breeze that day far from the land; but in the night, out on the main, there came a wind that whipped the sea to fury—the ship was driven to the land again and tossed against the rocks of the promontory. It sank, and so did most of what it carried; but a money-bag with three thousand silver drachmae inside was washed ashore and now is lying, covered with seaweed, close to a dead dolphin, for distaste of which no wayfarer has even gone near the spot, as all make haste to pass the stench of putrefaction. But *you* must approach, approach and lift up, lift up and give! For the present, it is enough that you should not seem poor; but hereafter you will be . . . rich!'

28. After giving this assurance, the Nymphs took their departure, receding with the shades of night. As soon as it was day, Daphnis leapt joyfully from his bed and drove his goats at a great pace to the pasture; he kissed Chloe, bowed low before the Nymphs' statues, and then went down to the sea, making the excuse that he wanted to sprinkle himself with holy water. He paced about on the sand close to where the waves were breaking, and kept a sharp lookout for the three thousand drachmae. There was no danger of his having to search for long, because the dolphin's evil smell assailed his nostrils, where it lay beached and oozing. With the rotting carcass to guide him, he quickly came to the place, scraped away the seaweed, and found the bag, which was still full of money. He picked it up and dropped it into his knapsack. And he did not go away from there until he had blessed the Nymphs and the very sea itself. For, although he was a goatherd, he now regarded the sea as a kinder friend than the land, because it was helping to bring about his marriage with Chloe.

29. Once in possession of the three thousand drachmae, Daphnis delayed no longer, but, thinking himself the richest of all men, and not merely of the local peasantry, he at once went to

Chloe and recounted his dream to her; he showed her the bag of money, told her to mind their animals until he came back, fairly sprinted to Dryas, and, on finding him threshing some wheat with Nape, plunged with indecent haste into the subject of marriage:

'Give me Chloe for my wife! I know how to play the pan-pipes well and prune a vine and dig-in fruit-trees; and I know how to plough the land and let the wind blow the chaff from the wheat. And Chloe can tell you how I tend a herd—fifty she-goats was what I took over, but I've made them twice as many; and I've bred fine big billy-goats, whereas we used to get the nannies served by other people's billies. Plus I'm young and I'm your neighbour and there's never been any bad blood between us, and a she-goat suckled me, just as a ewe suckled Chloe. So I'm that much better than the others, and neither will my gifts be worse than theirs— *they'll* give you goats and sheep and a yoke of mangy oxen and grain that you couldn't even feed hens on, but from me please accept these three thousand drachmae. Only no one must know about this, not even my father Lamon himself.'

With that he handed the bag to Dryas, flung his arms round him, and kissed him.

30. When, quite unexpectedly, Dryas and Nape beheld such a substantial sum of money, they promised to give him Chloe immediately, and undertook to get Lamon's consent to the marriage. Nape stayed behind with Daphnis, and went on driving the oxen round and round the threshing-floor and working over the ears of wheat with the *tribola*.* Dryas, however, put the money-bag away in the safe place where he kept Chloe's birth-tokens, and then hurried off to Lamon and Myrtale; he had in mind to do something unheard of—go a-wooing for a *bridegroom*! He caught them busy at much the same kind of job, measuring out barley which had been winnowed not long before, and in low spirits because the grain came close to being less than the seed they had sown. Refusing to let them be despondent over this, Dryas declared that the same tale of scarcity was being heard on all sides, and then went on to ask if he could have Daphnis for Chloe; he would take nothing from them, he said, although other suitors were offering plenty—on the contrary, he would give them something out of his own pocket by way of a dowry. The marriage made sense, he continued, because Daphnis and Chloe had been brought up with one another, and their herding had joined them in a friendship which would not easily be put asunder; moreover, they were now old enough to sleep together. All this and more did Dryas say, because he stood to be three thousand to the good if his plea were successful.

Lamon could no longer shelter behind his own poverty (since the other side was not taking a lofty tone) or behind Daphnis' youth (because he was of an age to marry); even so, he still kept to himself what he was really thinking—that Daphnis was too good for such a marriage—and, after a few moments' silence, made the following answer:

31. 'You do right in giving your neighbours preference over strangers, and in being disinclined to think more highly of wealth than of honest poverty. May Pan and the Nymphs love you for this! I, too, for my part, am desirous of this marriage—it would be foolish of me, now that I'm getting on in years and needing an extra hand or two on the farm, if I were not to accept the friendly assistance of your house, which would be a great blessing. And heaven knows that Chloe is a girl to die for!—she has beauty and youth and every virtue. But there is a stumbling-block: I'm a slave, and nothing that I have is mine to dispose of. My master must be told of this, and he must give his consent. So I propose that we postpone the wedding until the autumn—we keep getting word from town that he's coming then. That's when they'll be husband and wife; and in the meantime they can love each other like a brother and sister. Only, Dryas, be clear about one thing: he's a long way above us, that young man you're trying for.'

When Lamon had delivered himself thus, he kissed Dryas and—since it was now torrid noon—provided him with something to drink. And finally he accompanied him some distance on his way home, taking care to show him every possible courtesy.

32. The last sentence of Lamon's speech had made Dryas prick up his ears, and as he walked along he gave his mind to the question of who Daphnis was.

'He was fed by a she-goat, as though the gods were protecting him, and he's a handsome lad, and not a bit like that pug-nosed old gaffer and his bald-pate of a wife. *And* he was good for three thousand drachmae—you wouldn't expect a goatherd to have that many wild-pears! Can it be that Daphnis was abandoned by someone in the way that Chloe was? and that Lamon found Daphnis just as I found her? and that there were tokens beside him like the ones that I discovered? If all this is so, O Pan our Lord and Nymphs that we adore, maybe Daphnis will find his true parents, and that will give us a clue to the mystery of Chloe's birth.'

So Dryas mused and dreamed, all the way back to the threshing-floor. When he reached it, he found Daphnis on tip-toe for news, and electrified him by hailing him as his son-in-law; and then he promised to celebrate the marriage in the autumn, and gave his right hand as a pledge that Chloe would belong to Daphnis and no one else.

33. Quicker than thought, without stopping for food or drink, Daphnis sped back to Chloe. He found her busy with milking and cheese-making, and told her the glad tidings about their marriage. From then on he kissed her openly, as if she were his wife, and shared in her work: he would draw the milk into pails, set the cheeses to dry in wicker baskets, and put the lambs and the kids to their mothers. When these tasks had been properly seen to, they washed, had a quick snack and a cup of something, and then took a stroll to look for ripe fruit. There was no lack of this, because it was the season when Nature is most lavish: there were wild pears and garden pears and apples galore, of which some had already fallen down, and some were still on the trees, the ones on the ground being more fragrant, the ones on the branches more flawless in their bloom—the windfalls smelt like wine, the others glowed like gold. There stood an apple-tree, all picked, with neither fruit nor leaf remaining; bare were all its boughs; yet one apple* still hung ripening atop the very topmost twig, an apple large and lovely, which by itself surpassed the sweet scent of its whole clan. He feared to go up there, the harvester, nor had he taken heed to reach it down—perhaps some power was guarding it, that apple fair, for a love-struck shepherd.

34. When Daphnis saw the apple, he made to go up and pluck it, and took no notice of Chloe when she tried to hold him back. Whereupon she, ignored, went angrily away to the sheep and goats; but Daphnis quickly clambered up the tree and succeeded in plucking the apple and bringing it down as a gift for Chloe, and made this speech to the wrathful girl:

'O maiden,
this apple
　　the lovely Seasons of the Year brought forth
　　and a fair tree fed
　　beneath the mellowing Sun
　　and Chance preservèd;
and, while I have eyes, I am not the one to leave it there
that it may fall to earth
　　for browsing beast to trample
　　or gliding snake to poison
　　or Time to ruin when it lies forlorn—
　　the cynosure,
　　the nonpareil.
　　This did Aphrodite win as a prize for beauty,*
　　this do I give you as a prize of victory.
Like witnesses have you both:
　　Paris was a shepherd,
　　a goatherd am I.'

With these words he placed the apple in her bosom, and when he came close she kissed him, so that Daphnis was not sorry that he had risked climbing to such a height. For the kiss that he got was better than even a golden apple.

BOOK 4

1. There now came from Mytilene a fellow-slave of Lamon's, who told them that their master would be arriving shortly before the grape-harvest in order to find out for himself whether his estate had suffered any damage in the Methymnaean raid. Since summer was already nearing its end and autumn was not far off, Lamon at once began to prepare the guest's lodging in a way that would give his senses every pleasure—he cleaned out the springs, to make sure that the water in them would be pure, carried the muck out of the farmyard, so that its smell would not offend, and tidied up the pleasure-ground,* so that it would be a delight to the eye.

2. This pleasure-ground was a place of rare beauty, and fit to grace the palace of an emperor. It was situated on an eminence, and measured a stade in length and four plethra* in breadth; its appearance was that of an extensive plain. All kinds of trees grew there*—apple-trees, myrtles, pear-trees and pomegranate-trees and fig-trees and olives. High up on one side was a vine; its grapes were just darkening to purple, and it overhung the apple-trees and pear-trees, as though disputing with them about which had the better fruit. Besides these cultivated trees, there were also cypresses and laurels and plane-trees and pine-trees, which all supported ivy instead of the vine, and the clusters of ivy-berries were large and turning black, so that they imitated bunches of grapes. The fruit-trees were on the inside, as though for safe-keeping; the barren ones surrounded them on the outside like a man-made fence; and round them in turn ran a narrow circuit-wall of dry stones. All was divided and apportioned, and tree-trunk kept its distance from tree-trunk; overhead, however, the branches came together and interwove their leaves—this happened naturally, but it looked as though human skill had been at work. There were flower-beds, too, some furnished by the earth, some made by art; the gardener had planted the rose-beds, the hyacinths and the lilies, but the soil unaided sent up violets and

narcissi and pimpernels. There was shade in summer, in spring there were flowers, in autumn grapes, and no season was without its fruits.

3. From there, a wide prospect opened over the plain and the sea beyond, and it was possible to see the peasants minding their flocks and herds, and the ships scudding across the bay—that view was another of the delights afforded by the pleasure-ground. At the point where the length and breadth of this paradise found their exact centre, there stood a temple and an altar of Dionysus. The altar was mantled in ivy, the temple in vine-branches. Inside, the temple had paintings of the Dionysus-story—Semele giving him birth,* Ariadne sleeping, Lycurgus bound, Pentheus being torn asunder. The god's conquest of the Indians was there, and how he changed the Tyrrhenian pirates into dolphins. Everywhere were Satyrs treading grapes, everywhere were Maenads dancing. Nor was Pan forgotten, but he, too, was portrayed, sitting on a rock and playing his pipes, as though making music for grape-treaders and dancers alike.

4. Such was the pleasure-ground, and Lamon now set to work there, taking out the dead growth and tying up the vine-branches. He put a garland on the statue of Dionysus, and brought water to the flowers along an irrigation-ditch, leading it from a spring that Daphnis had discovered for this very purpose—the spring was reserved for the flowers, but everyone called it 'Daphnis' Spring'. Lamon also told Daphnis to feed up the goats as much as he could, warning him that their master was bound to include the herd in his tour of inspection after so long an absence. Daphnis had no misgivings on that score—he was expecting praise for the way he had looked after the goats, because he had doubled their number and had not lost a single one to the wolves, and they were fatter than the sheep; but he wanted to get his master's blessing for his marriage, and that caused him to put forth all his care and enthusiasm on his animals. He led them out to pasture at the very crack of dawn, and kept them there until the evening; he took them down to drink twice a day, and sought out the places that offered the best grazing. He made new bowls and lots of milk-pails, and set up bigger baskets for drying the cheeses on. So

thorough were his preparations that he even oiled the goats'
horns and combed their hair—you would have taken them for
Pan's own sacred flock. All his work on them was shared by
Chloe, who neglected her sheep and gave most of her time to the
goats—making Daphnis think that *she* was the reason why they
looked so beautiful!

5. While they were busy with these tasks, there came a second
messenger from the town, who instructed them to lose no time in
gathering the fruit from the vines, and said that he would stay
with them until they had made the grapes into new wine, after
which he would go back to town and bring their master—that
would be at the end of the autumn vintage-time. They welcomed
this Eudromus* (that was his name) with all due hospitality, and
got on with picking the grapes: they brought the bunches to the
wine-presses, carried the grape-juice to the storage-jars, and set
aside the most luxuriant clusters, still hanging from the branches,
so that when the visitors arrived from town, they might be able
to picture the vintage for themselves and enjoy some of its
pleasures.

6. When Eudromus was all ready to stride out on his way back
to town, Daphnis pressed on him an assortment of gifts, including
some samples of what his herd produced: firmly set cheeses,
a late-born kid, and a shaggy, white goatskin for him to put on
over his clothes when he was on running-duty in wintertime.
Eudromus was delighted with his presents, and he kissed Daphnis
and promised to say something nice about him to their master.

And then he went away full of goodwill. But Daphnis was
uneasy as he pastured his goats with Chloe, and Chloe was dis-
mayed to think that, young as Daphnis was, and used to seeing
only his goats and the mountain and the peasants and her, he was
about to have his first interview with his master, a personage
unknown to him hitherto except by name. And so she brooded
anxiously about Daphnis, wondering what he would say when he
came into the great man's presence. The thought of her marriage,
too, filled her with dread—was it not likely that they were both
dreaming of something that could never be? They kissed and
kissed, therefore, as though they would never stop, and clung

together as though fused into a single body. Yet their kisses were fearful and their embraces joyless, as if their master had already come and they were trembling before him or trying to hide from his face. And now a fresh cause of anxiety befell them.

7. There was a cowherd called Lampis, a conceited fellow. He was one of Chloe's suitors, and he had already loaded Dryas with presents in his eagerness for the marriage. When, therefore, he realized that Daphnis was sure to marry Chloe if their master's permission was forthcoming, he tried to think of a scheme for putting the master against the lovers. Lampis knew that the landowner was particularly fond of his pleasure-ground, and this decided him to do all he could to spoil the place and rob it of its beauty. Were he to cut down the trees, he was bound to be caught because of the noise. And so he concentrated on vandalizing the flower-beds—waiting for night and climbing over the wall, he proceeded to dig up some plants, snap the stems of others, and trample hog-like over the rest. Then he crept away, having been seen by no one. Next morning Lamon came into the garden with the intention of watering the flowers from the spring; but when he saw the place all ruined, and a scene of havoc that was clearly the work of an ill-wisher and no pirate, he straightaway tore his tunic and called loudly on the gods to be his witnesses. The commotion made Myrtale drop her housework and come running out of the cottage, while Daphnis left his goats and raced to Lamon's side. They took one look and cried out in anguish, and as they cried out their tears rolled down, and there was mourning of a kind unknown before—for flowers!

8. True, they were weeping for fear of their master; but even a complete stranger would have wept, had he chanced on such a sight. For the place had been shorn of its charm, and all the earth was turned now to mud. Here and there a flower had escaped the onslaught—beneath the wreckage it bloomed and glowed and was still fair, although brought low; the bees were alighting on these remnants, and their droning, which had neither pause nor end, was like a wail of lamentation. As for Lamon, despair wrung from him this outburst:

'Oh, my rose-bed!
    it's all broken down, just look at it!
Oh, my violets!
    all of them trampled in the mire!
Oh, my hyacinths and my narcissi!
    some fiend of a man has dug them up!
Next spring will come,
    but they'll not flower;
the summer will be here,
    but no fine show of blooms;
and then another autumn,
    but they won't garland anyone.
Lord Dionysus, how came it that even you felt no pity for
        these poor flowers,
when they were your neighbours
and you saw them every day
and I crowned you with them so often?
How will I dare to show the garden to my master *now*?
And how will he be minded when he sees it?
He'll hoist my ancient carcass on a pine, just like Apollo
        did to Marsyas*—
and Daphnis, too, perhaps, because he'll say he has the
        goats to thank for this!'

9. At Lamon's words their tears fell hotter still, and now it was their own skins, and not the flowers, that they were grieving for. Chloe grieved, too, at the thought of Daphnis hanging aloft; she prayed that their master would cancel his journey, and dragged out the days in misery, as though she could already see Daphnis writhing under the lash. When darkness was just beginning to fall, Eudromus brought them news that their master—the elder one, that is—intended to arrive in three days' time, but that his son was coming in advance, and would be with them next day. This made them think hard about the situation, and they invited Eudromus to help them decide what was to be done. He was well disposed towards Daphnis, and his advice was that they should confess the occurrence first to the young master—Eudromus undertook to be their advocate, because he was the young man's foster-brother, and highly esteemed by him. When the next day came, they did exactly as Eudromus had advised.

10. Astylus* duly arrived, riding on a horse, and with him came a crony of the sort called 'parasite'* who was also on horseback. Astylus was just beginning to have down on his chin, but Gnathon* (that was the parasite's name) was long past the time when his beard had first felt the razor. Lamon fell down before his master's feet, together with Myrtale and Daphnis. 'Have mercy on an unfortunate old man!' begged he. 'Deliver from your father's wrath one who is innocent of any crime!' And he accompanied this plea with a full account of what had happened. Astylus took pity on their entreaties, and went forward to the pleasure-ground; when he saw the devastation in the flower-garden, he promised to intercede with his father and tell him that the horses were the culprits—he would say that they had been tethered there but had pranced about until they freed themselves, after which they had broken some of the flowers, trampled on others, and uprooted the rest. At this, Lamon and Myrtale called down heaven's blessings on his head, while Daphnis fetched him gifts of kids, cheeses, hens and chickens, grapes on the vine-branch and apples on the bough. One of the gifts was fragrant wine*—Lesbian wine is the most delicious of drinks.

11. Astylus stayed just long enough to say 'Thank you', and then he was off for a spot of hare-hunting—a suitable pastime for a rich youngster who lived for pleasure and had come to the country in order to find new ways of enjoying himself. Gnathon, though, was a creature who knew how to guzzle and booze and play the satyr in his cups, and there was nothing to him but a pair of jaws and a belly and the apparatus under his belly. So the sight of Daphnis bearing his gifts was not lost on him—he was a pederast by temperament, and here was beauty of an order that he had never seen in the town. He decided, therefore, to make a pass at Daphnis, and anticipated no problems in getting his way with a mere goatherd. Resolved on this, he absented himself from Astylus' hunting expedition, and instead went down to where Daphnis was herding, ostensibly to look at the goats, but really to

run his eye over Daphnis. By way of softening him up, he com-
plimented him on his goats, and made him play the goatherds'
tune on his pipes; he also threw in a promise to get him his
freedom before long, claiming to have unlimited influence.

12. After he had seen Daphnis all tame and trusting, he lay in
wait for him that night as he drove the goats back from pasture—
running up to Daphnis, he first kissed him and then asked him to
do for him what the she-goats do for the he-goats. Daphnis took a
moment or two to realize what he meant; and then he answered
that it was right for the he-goats to mount the she-goats, but
nobody ever saw a he-goat mounting a he-goat or a ram mounting
another ram instead of the tups or cocks treading cocks instead of
the hens. Whereupon Gnathon tried to seize hold of him, intent
on nothing less than rape. But Daphnis gave him a shove that sent
him sprawling on the ground (the fellow was drunk and unsteady
on his feet) and then scampered away like a puppy, leaving him to
lie there—a *man's* hand, not a boy's, was what Gnathon needed to
guide him home. Henceforth, Daphnis would not allow the parasite anywhere near him, but pastured his goats in a different place
each day, keeping well clear of Gnathon, and taking good care of
Chloe. As for Gnathon, he wasted no more of his time once he
had learned that Daphnis was as sturdy as he was handsome. But
he kept watching for an opportunity to mention him to Astylus,
and hoped that he would yet have Daphnis as a present from the
young man, who was ready to indulge his every whim.

13. For the time being, however, there was nothing he could
do, because Dionysophanes and his wife Cleariste* were arriving,
and there was a tremendous hubbub of mules and slaves and men
and women. But later he made up a long, sentimental oration on
the subject.

At this season of his life, Dionysophanes' black hair was flecked
with grey, but he was tall and handsome and strong enough to be
a match for young men half his age. Moreover, there were few as
wealthy as he, and none as noble-hearted. When he came, he
sacrificed on that first day to the gods who preside over
agriculture—Demeter and Dionysus and Pan and the Nymphs—
and supplied a big bowl of wine for everyone present to help

themselves from. On the succeeding days he made his inspection of Lamon's work on the farm; and when he saw the fields newly furrowed and the vines stripped down to the wood and the pleasure-ground restored to its beauty (all blame for the trampled flowers having been put right by Astylus), he was vastly pleased, and praised Lamon, and promised to give him his freedom. Next, he went down to the pasture to see the goats and their goatherd.

14. The approach of such a throng of people was too much for Chloe—overawed and unnerved, she fled into the wood. But Daphnis stood his ground undaunted; he was wearing a shaggy goatskin, belted at the waist, and a leather haversack, its stitching brand new, was hanging by a strap from his shoulders; both his hands held gifts—he carried freshly made cheeses in one, while two suckling kids rested on his other forearm. If Apollo ever herded cattle* in King Laomedon's service, surely he looked as Daphnis did that day! He himself said nothing, but blushed crimson as, with downcast eyes, he held out his gifts. Lamon, though, spoke up:

'May it please you, master,' said he, 'this is the keeper of your honour's goats. Fifty of them did you give me to pasture, and two billies; but he has made them a hundred, and ten billies. Do you see how sleek they are, and how thick are their coats, and how unbroken their horns? He's made them musical too—at least, they do everything to the sound of his pan-pipes.'

15. Now, Cleariste was there when Lamon said this, and she took a notion to test the truth of his claim; she told Daphnis to pipe to the goats as he usually did, and promised to present him with a tunic and a cloak and a pair of shoes when he had finished. Nothing loath, Daphnis made the company sit round, just like the audience in a theatre; then he went and stood beneath the oak-tree, opened his haversack, and took out his pipes. He began by breathing into them very softly, which caused the goats to raise their heads and stand still; then he played the tune which was the signal for grazing, and the goats lowered their heads and began to feed; then he sounded a high and dulcet note, whereat they all lay down as one; the next tune he piped had a somewhat shrill and piercing tone, and the animals reacted to it by fleeing into the

forest, as though a wolf were coming; after a minute or two he
sounded the return, and they came bounding from the shelter of
the trees and gathered together in front of where he stood. For
obedience to their master's command, you would not have found
even a troop of human slaves the equal of these goats! Everyone
was astonished, and nobody more than Cleariste, who vowed to
give this handsome and harmonious goatherd his promised
reward. After this, the visitors went up to the farm and took their
luncheon, sending Daphnis a share of what they were eating.
Daphnis ate his picnic with Chloe—he was delighted with his
taste of the fine city-fare, and his hopes ran high that he would be
able to win over his masters and bring his marriage to pass.

16. Gnathon's passion had been further inflamed by the ex-
hibition that Daphnis had given with his goats, and he felt that
life would be unbearable if he were not to possess him. Waiting,
therefore, until he saw Astylus sauntering in the pleasure-ground,
he led him up into the temple of Dionysus and began kissing his
feet and hands. Astylus asked Gnathon the reason for this
behaviour, said that he must tell him all, and vowed to help him.

'Oh master,' exclaimed the other, 'it's all up with your
Gnathon now! Remember how the only thing I loved was your
table spread for dinner, and how I swore that there was no treat
like a bottle of old wine, and how I reckoned more to your chefs
than to the prettiest boys in Mytilene—well, I'm finished with all
that; from now on, nothing looks good to me but Daphnis! And
you can keep your expensive food, because I won't touch it, in
spite of all that roast meat they get ready every day, and all the
fish and pastries—but I'd willingly be a goat and eat grass and
leaves if I could hear the sound of Daphnis' pipes and be herded
by him. Oh master, save your Gnathon, and conquer Love the
Conqueror! Because if you won't, I swear by your own self (for
you're my god, you know) that I'll take a dagger and then I'll fill
my stomach full and then I'll KILL myself on Daphnis' doorstep,
and you'll never call me your little Jaw-Jaw again, like you used to
when you were having a lark!'

17. Now Astylus was a generous-natured youth, and he was
not unacquainted with the sorrows of love on his own account;

and so when Gnathon began blubbing and making another assault on his feet he could not find it in his heart to refuse him, but promised to ask his father for Daphnis and carry him off to town as his own slave and Gnathon's darling. But he did make one attempt to touch the conscience of that hardened sinner, asking him with a disarming smile 'Wasn't he ashamed of being in love with Lamon's son, and did he really want to go to bed with a boy who herded goats?'—and he simulated disgust at the unpleasant smell of these animals. Gnathon, however, had been schooled in the whole mythology of love while roistering with his ne'er-do-well friends in Mytilene, and he was ready with an able defence of himself and Daphnis:

'Master, no lover allows *that* sort of thing to put him off, but he's beauty's captive no matter what shape he finds it inhabiting. That's why people have been known to fall in love with a tree, or a river, or a beast—yet who wouldn't pity a lover who needed to *fear* the object of his affections? In my own case, I love the body of a slave, but the beauty of a free man. Do you see how his hair is like the hyacinth and his eyes shine beneath his temples with the light of gem-stones in a golden setting? and how his face is tinged all over with blushing crimson and his mouth is arrayed with teeth as white as ivory? What lover would not long to take sweet kisses from that mouth? And if I've fallen for a herd-boy, I'm only doing what the gods did: Anchises was a cow-herd, yet Aphrodite took him as her lover; Branchus herded goats, and Apollo kissed him;* Ganymede was a shepherd, and the Lord of All* carried him off to heaven. Do not speak slightingly, Astylus, of a boy whom we saw the very goats obeying as though they were in love with him, but let us rather return thanks to Zeus' eagles for permitting beauty so rare to walk the earth unmolested!'

18. Astylus shook with mirth when he heard Gnathon's peroration. 'Thus passion doth make sophists of us all!' he chortled. Nevertheless, he began to watch for an opportunity of speaking to his father about Daphnis.

Now, Eudromus had heard all this from a dark corner of the temple; he liked Daphnis, whom he considered a decent lad, and it grieved him to think of such beauty being put at the mercy of

Gnathon's drunken brutality. Without a moment's delay, therefore, he informed Daphnis and Lamon about the whole plot.
Daphnis was thunderstruck: his first thought was to screw up his
courage and run away with Chloe or to make her join him in a
suicide-pact. But Lamon told Myrtale to come outside the yard
with him, and spoke urgently to her:

'God help us, wife! The time has come for us to uncover our
secret. From this day forth you and I will be without a son, and
the goats and everything else will be forlorn—but, by Pan and the
Nymphs, I'm not going to keep quiet about Daphnis' history, not
even if they abandon me like the old ox in its stall! I'll tell them
that I found him left to die, and I'll say just how I found him
being kept alive, and I'll show them what I found lying beside
him. That pervert Gnathon had better know what kind of boy
he's trying to get his clammy hands on! Just keep the tokens
handy for when I need them.'

19. As soon as the old couple had agreed on this plan, they
went back indoors. And now Astylus attached himself to his
father when he saw him at leisure, and begged for leave to take
Daphnis back to town with him, because he was good-looking
and above peasant life and could quickly be taught by Gnathon to
behave the way they do in cities. His father cheerfully consented:
there and then he sent for Lamon and Myrtale, and gave them the
glad tidings that Daphnis was to be the servant of Astylus in
future, and not of nanny-goats and billy-goats; and he promised
to give them two goatherds in place of him. By this time the slaves
had all come thronging round, and there was general rejoicing at
the prospect of this handsome new recruit. Amid the excitement,
Lamon asked if he might speak, and began as follows:

'Hearken, master, to a true story from an old man's lips; and I
swear by Pan and the Nymphs that I will tell you no lie.

'I am not the father of Daphnis, nor did Myrtale ever have the
good fortune to be a mother. Other parents left this child to his
fate—maybe they had older children, as many as they wanted—
and I found him lying abandoned, and my she-goat giving him
suck; when that goat died, I buried her in the garden of my
cottage, because I loved her for doing what a mother should have

done. I found tokens, too, lying there beside the baby (I admit it, master), and I still have them in a safe place, because they point to a station in life far above our own. Now master, don't misjudge me—I don't think it beneath Daphnis to wait upon Astylus; he'd be a good servant, and the young master's a real gentleman. But I can't stand by and see him turned into Gnathon's plaything—that drunken beast wants to get Daphnis to Mytilene and make him his whore!'

20. Lamon stopped after he had said this, and his tears began to flow. Gnathon, on the other hand, blazed up with indignation and raised his fist to strike Lamon. But Dionysophanes, who had appeared strangely moved by Lamon's recital, told Gnathon to hold his tongue, glaring fiercely at him from under knitted brows. Then he took Lamon through his story again, warning him to tell the truth and not to invent fantasies in the hope of keeping his son. But Lamon was obdurate—he swore by all the gods, and offered to let himself be tortured as a test of whether he was deceiving them. Dionysophanes put Lamon's words on the rack instead, and Cleariste was at hand to help him judge, as he pondered thus:

'Why should Lamon want to tell lies when he stands to be given two goatherds for the one he's losing? And what motive could a peasant have had for inventing that tale?—surely it was incredible from the start that so fine a lad could have been brought into the world by that old man and a pauper-mother!'

21. He decided that his best course was not to speculate further, but then and there to look at the tokens and see whether they gave any hint of fame and fortune above the ordinary. Myrtale went to fetch the precious relics, which were all kept in an old leather bag. They were brought, and Dionysophanes took the first look. When he saw a little crimson cloak, a brooch of beaten gold, and an ivory-hilted dagger, he uttered a loud cry of 'O Zeus our Lord!' and made his wife come and see for herself. She looked inside the bag, and burst out in turn

'O blessed Fates! Surely these are what we put beside our son when we left him in the wild! Wasn't it these fields that we sent Sophrone* to carry him to? There's no doubt about the tokens—

these are the very ones! Dear husband, the boy is ours—Daphnis is your son, and he was herding his father's goats!'

22. Clearéste was in mid-speech, and Dionysophanes was still kissing the tokens and weeping in a transport of joy, when Astylus, realizing that Daphnis was his brother, flung off his cloak and went racing down from the pleasure-ground, eager to be the first to kiss him. But when Daphnis saw him pelting towards him at the head of a mob and calling out his name, he thought that Astylus was coming to seize him; and so he dropped his haversack and his pan-pipes, and ran off in the direction of the sea, intending to throw himself over the cliff. And perhaps Daphnis would have suffered the preposterous fate of finding his parents and losing his life in the same hour, had not Astylus grasped the situation and shouted again

'Stop, Daphnis, stop! Don't be afraid—I'm your brother . . . and your masters aren't your masters any more—they're your parents! Lamon has just told us about the she-goat and shown us the tokens. Turn round and look at their faces—they're beaming and laughing all the way! Come on, kiss me first—I'm not telling lies, I swear by the Nymphs I'm not!'

23. It was the oath that did the trick: Daphnis halted—though still reluctantly—and waited for Astylus to catch him up, and when he came, he embraced him. While Daphnis was kissing Astylus, the rest of the field came in—serving-men and serving-women, and his father himself, with his mother at his side. They all hugged and kissed Daphnis, and there was weeping and rejoicing. But Daphnis took his father and mother to his bosom before all the rest, and clung there as if he had known them for ages, and could not bring himself to quit their embrace. So quickly do we give our trust when Nature is the bond! For a short time he even forgot all about Chloe—that was while he went into the cottage, put on fine clothes, then sat down next to his very own father, and listened to him as he made the following speech:

24. 'I wed your mother, my sons, when I was still quite a young man, and in no very long time I had become a father, and thought myself a lucky fellow, because three children came along—a son first, a daughter second, and thirdly Astylus. After *problem?*

that, I thought my family was big enough; and when this boy was born in addition to all the others, I abandoned him to his fate—when I put these tokens beside him I thought of them not as means of recognition, but as offerings at his grave. But Fortune had other intentions; my elder son and my daughter were taken off by the same sickness in a single day, but you, Daphnis, were spared to me by the gods' providence, so that your mother and I may have more hands to care for us in our declining years. So don't bear me a grudge for having exposed you—I took that course much against my will. And don't let it vex *you*, Astylus, that you'll come in for a half-share of my property instead of the whole; because a brother is better than any material possession—any sensible person knows that. But love one another, both of you, and think yourselves as good as princes, so far as money goes! For I'll be leaving you all the land you could wish for, and a host of clever slaves, and gold and silver and everything else that rich men possess. The only exception is this estate, which I'm giving Daphnis, along with Lamon and Myrtale and the goats that he tended with the sweat of his own brow.'

25. He was still speaking, when up jumped Daphnis and exclaimed,

'It's a good job you reminded me, father—I'll go and take the goats for their drink; they'll be listening for my pipes now, and they must be thirsty, and I'm just sitting here!'

There was a burst of laughter at this—they all thought it exquisitely funny that Daphnis was still a goatherd after being promoted to master! Someone else was sent to see to the animals, and meanwhile the whole gathering sacrificed to Zeus the Saviour, and then settled down to enjoy a celebration. The only absentee was Gnathon, who spent that day and the next night skulking anxiously, like a suppliant, in the temple of Dionysus.

In no time at all the whole countryside had heard the rumour that Dionysophanes had found a son and Daphnis the goatherd was discovered to be lord of the estate. Next morning at dawn, people came flocking from all directions, to congratulate the young man and bring gifts to his father. First and foremost was Dryas, Chloe's foster-father.

26. After these visitors had partaken of his joy, Dionysophanes kept them all with him to partake of his feast as well. Floods of wine and mounds of wheat-flour had been provided, and there were waterfowl and sucking-pigs and every kind of dainty. Sacrifice, too, consisting of the burnt flesh of animals, was being offered in plenty to the local gods. Daphnis now got together all his herdsman's tackle and divided it into lots, for dedication to the gods—he dedicated his haversack and his goatskin to Dionysus, his pan-pipes and his flute to Pan, and his crook and his home-made milk-pails to the Nymphs. But familiar things have a charm that is not eclipsed by unwonted prosperity; and Daphnis wept over each of these dear possessions at parting—he did not dedicate the pails until he had drawn milk into them again, nor the goatskin until he had wrapped himself in it, nor his pan-pipes until he had played one last tune on them; besides that, he kissed all these offerings, and spoke to the she-goats, and called the billy-goats to him by name. As for the spring, he drank from it, because he had so often done that with Chloe. Still, however, he did not avow his love, but waited for an opportune moment.

27. While Daphnis was taken up with these ceremonies, Chloe fared as will now be told. She sat about weeping, minding her sheep, and saying the kind of thing that you would expect:

'Daphnis has quite forgotten me, and he's dreaming of marrying some rich girl—oh, why did I make him swear by the goats and not the Nymphs? He's forsaken his goats and Chloe too. Even when he was sacrificing to the Nymphs and Pan, he didn't want to see Chloe. Maybe he's found fancier girls than me among his mother's waiting-women. Well, let him go or let him tarry—but I can't endure life any longer!'   *(66)*

28. As Chloe whimpered and moped like this, Lampis the cowherd* suddenly appeared with a band of yokels and carried her off—he reckoned that Daphnis would not be marrying her now, and that Dryas would be happy to have him as a son-in-law. And so she was borne away, uttering screams that would have drawn pity from a stone; but there were witnesses of the abduction, and one of them told Nape, who told Dryas, who told Daphnis. He was beside himself at the news—not daring to speak to his father about it, and yet unable to bear the blow in silence, he went out into the garden of the cottage and gave vent to his sorrow:

'Much good it's done me to find my parents! How much better it was for me to be a goatherd, and how much happier I was when I was a slave! I could see Chloe then, and hear Chloe's voice. But now Lampis has stolen her and got clean away, and when night comes he'll take her to bed. And here am I drinking and feasting, and the oaths I swore by Pan and the goats were just moonshine!'

29. Every word of this was overheard by Gnathon as he lay hidden in the pleasure-ground, and it occurred to him that he had been given a fine opportunity to put things right between himself and Daphnis. Quickly assembling a troop of Astylus' young serving-men, he sought out Dryas and made him lead the way to Lampis' cottage. Then he ran there as fast as he could, caught Lampis in the very act of leading Chloe inside, took possession of the girl, and thrashed the unfortunate rustics. Gnathon meant to follow this up by marching Lampis away in bonds, like a captive taken in war—but Lampis forestalled him by running away. With this famous victory to his credit, Gnathon came home at nightfall; he found Dionysophanes already asleep, but Daphnis was awake and still sobbing in the cottage-garden. He led Chloe up to Daphnis, handed her over, and related everything that had passed. Then he put two requests to Daphnis—that he should forget the past and accept the services of a slave who could be of much use to him, and that he should not ban Gnathon from his table, because that would be condemning him to death by starvation. One look at Chloe, one moment with Chloe in his arms, and Daphnis was reconciled to his parasite-benefactor, while he stammered out an apology to Chloe for his neglect of her.

30. When they came to consider their next step, it seemed best for them to conceal their marriage-plans, and for Daphnis to keep Chloe well out of the public eye, making his love known to no one but his mother Cleariste. But Dryas would have none of this—he insisted on speaking to Daphnis' father, and guaranteed to win him over without help from anyone else. Early the next morning, therefore, he put Chloe's birth-tokens in his haversack and approached Dionysophanes and Cleariste as they sat in the pleasure-ground with Astylus and Daphnis himself beside them. Dryas waited for silence to fall, and then began to speak.

'A like necessity to Lamon's obliges me to speak of things which have remained unuttered until now. Chloe here is not my daughter, nor did I rear her in her earliest infancy, but she had other parents, and a ewe fed her as she lay abandoned in the cave of the Nymphs. I saw this with my own eyes, and wondered at the sight, and went from wondering to fostering. If you need proof, there is her beauty (for she's not a bit like us), and there are the tokens (for they're more costly than a shepherd could afford). Look at that evidence, then search for the girl's family—let's see whether she may yet seem worthy of Daphnis!'

31. The last few words of Dryas' speech were not let slip without a purpose, and Dionysophanes did not fail to listen to them attentively. He glanced at Daphnis, saw him turn pale and wipe away a secret tear, and knew immediately that the youth was in love; then, concerned more for his own son than for someone else's daughter, he questioned Dryas very strictly about what he had just said. But when he saw the tokens that had been brought—the gold-decorated sandals, the ankle-rings, the headband—he sent for Chloe and told her not to fret, because she already had a husband, and it would not be long before she found her father and her mother. Then Chloe was taken into the care of Cleariste, who from that day on dressed her in a style befitting the wife of her son. Daphnis, meanwhile, was made by Dionysophanes to stand up and answer the single question, 'Is Chloe a virgin?' And when Daphnis swore that matters had not gone beyond kissing and oath-taking, Dionysophanes expressed himself well pleased, and made them all take their places for his party.

32. And now they were able to appreciate what beauty can be when it is set off by tasteful adornment. For when Chloe had put on a robe, done up her hair in braids, and washed her face, she seemed to them all so much lovelier that Daphnis himself scarcely recognized her. Even without the tokens, you would have sworn that such a girl did not have Dryas for her father. But Dryas was present in spite of that, sharing in the feast with Nape,

and beside them, on a dining-couch of their own, were Lamon and Myrtale. In the days that followed, more animals were sacrificed to the gods, more bowls of wine were set down, and Chloe, in her turn, dedicated her own gear—her pan-pipes, her haversack, her goatskin, and her milk-pails. She also poured an offering of wine into the spring that welled up in the cave, because she had been suckled by its side and had often bathed in its waters. And she laid garlands on the ewe's grave, which Dryas pointed out to her, and piped a farewell tune to her flock, as Daphnis had done, and, at its close, prayed to the goddesses that those who had abandoned her would turn out to be not too humble for her marriage to Daphnis.

33. When the delights of making holiday in the country had begun to pall, they decided to go to town, look for Chloe's parents, and put off the wedding no longer. Bright and early, therefore, they packed up and made their parting-gifts. Dryas was given another three thousand drachmae; but on Lamon they bestowed half the estate, for him to harvest the grain and gather the fruit, plus the goats and goatherds, and four yokes of oxen, and clothes for the winter. And they made him a free man and his wife a free woman. After that, they journeyed to Mytilene by horse and ox-cart, borne in luxury. They arrived after dark, and so were not seen by the citizens at the time. Next day, however, a crowd gathered round their doors, women as well as men. The men were eager to congratulate Dionysophanes on finding a son—the more so when they saw how handsome Daphnis was; while the women wanted to rejoice with Cl=eariste because she was bringing home a son and a bride at one and the same time—for Chloe's peerless beauty dazzled them as Daphnis had dazzled their husbands. And so the whole town was abuzz over the youth and the girl; everyone pronounced them enviable already in their marriage, and prayed that the girl's parentage, when found, would prove to be worthy of her beauty. And more than one billionairess implored the gods that she might be credited with being the mother of so fair a daughter.

34. All this palaver gave Dionysophanes plenty to think about, and afterwards he sank into a deep sleep and had the following

dream. He seemed to see the Nymphs begging Love to give his consent, at long last, for the marriage of Daphnis and Chloe; at which the god unstrung his little bow and laid aside his quiver and commanded Dionysophanes to invite all the foremost citizens of Mytilene to a banquet, and, when he had filled the last mixing-bowl, to show each and every guest Chloe's recognition-tokens, and, after that, to sing the wedding-hymn. Fresh from seeing and hearing these things in his dream, Dionysophanes rose at dawn and ordered his servants to prepare a magnificent banquet from the choicest delicacies obtainable by land or sea, in lake or river. And then he invited all the grandees of Mytilene to dine with him. They feasted until nightfall; and when the mixing-bowl had been filled for the customary offering to Hermes,* a servant brought in the tokens on a silver salver, and showed them to everyone, carrying them round the company from left to right.

35. To all the guests but one the tokens meant nothing. The exception was a certain Megacles, who occupied the last place* on account of his old age—he knew the tokens at a glance, and exclaimed in a loud, vigorous voice

'What do I see here? O my daughter!—what has become of you? Are you alive, like Daphnis, or did some shepherd stumble on these, and these alone, and carry them off? I beg of you, Dionysophanes, tell me how those emblems of my child came into your hands—you've got Daphnis, so don't grudge *me* a lucky find as well!'

But Dionysophanes told him to say first of all where and in what circumstances the child had been exposed. Megacles replied thus, abating none of his vehemence:

'There was a time, long ago now, when I was very hard up—for I had spent everything that I possessed on financing choruses and fitting out triremes.* When my affairs were in that state, my wife presented me with a daughter. I wasn't eager to bring up the child in poverty, and so I exposed it, leaving these trinkets with it by way of recognition-tokens; I knew that there's no shortage of people anxious to become parents even by *those* means. Well, the baby was left in a grotto of the Nymphs, entrusted to the goddesses. But as for me, money began rolling in to me daily—and there I was without anyone to leave it to! By that time, you see, it was more than I could do to father a daughter, far less a son and heir. But it seems as though the gods are wanting to make a fool of me now, because they keep sending me dreams every night and telling me that I'm going to be made a father by (you'll never credit this)* . . . by a sheep!'

36. At this, Dionysophanes let out a roar far louder than Megacles' exclamation, and, leaping up, he went and brought in Chloe, who was dressed in the height of elegance. Then he addressed Megacles:

'This is the child that you exposed. This maiden did a sheep foster for you, by the gods' providence, just as a goat fostered Daphnis for me. Take them, your tokens and your daughter— and, having taken, give her back again to Daphnis as his bride. We abandoned them both, we have found them both, and both were cherished by Pan, the Nymphs, and Love.'*

This speech was warmly commended by Megacles, who sent for his wife Rhoda* and pressed Chloe to his bosom. And then they settled down to sleep, without shifting from their places; for Daphnis vowed that he would surrender Chloe to no one—not even to her father himself.

37. When the next day came, they all with one accord set off back to the country; this was at the request of Daphnis and Chloe, who were not taking kindly to life in the town—but their elders, too, had decided to give them a shepherd-style wedding. After arriving at Lamon's, therefore, they brought Dryas to meet Megacles, made Nape acquainted with Rhoda, and began to prepare on a lavish scale for the wedding-feast. Then Chloe's father gave the bride away, standing before the Nymphs in their grotto, and dedicated to them the birth-tokens and many other offerings. To Dryas he gave what was needed to make his reward up to ten thousand silver drachmae.

38. The weather was fine, and so Dionysophanes spread couches of greenery right in front of the cave, invited all the villagers to recline at their ease, and fed them royally, with no expense spared. Among the guests were Lamon and Myrtale, Dryas and Nape, Dorcon's relatives, Philetas, the sons of

Philetas, and Chromis and Lycaenion. Even Lampis was forgiven and allowed to attend. As was natural in such a company, everything was rustic and countrified: someone gave a rendering of the songs sung at reaping and mowing, and someone else cracked the kind of jokes that fly back and forth over the wine-press. Philetas obliged with his pan-pipes, Lampis favoured with his flute. Dryas and Lamon danced, Daphnis and Chloe kissed and cuddled. And meanwhile the goats cropped the grass nearby, as though they, too, were sharing in the feast; the city-folk did not care much for *that*—but Daphnis, undeterred, called some of the goats to him by name and gave them leafy twigs to eat, after which he took each one by the horns and kissed it!

39. That was not the end of their rustic idyll, but all their days Daphnis and Chloe lived like shepherds as often as not, worshipping the Nymphs and Pan and Love as their particular gods, possessing flocks of sheep and herds of goats in great number, and reckoning that no food was so delightful as milk and grapes and fruit of all kinds. They put their male-child under a she-goat as his wet-nurse, and when their second child, a daughter, was born, they made her suck the teats of a ewe; and they named their son Philopoemen* and their daughter Agele.* And so their shepherd-life grew old, as they themselves grew old.* And they beautified the cave, and set up pictures,* and established an altar to Love the Shepherd. And they let Pan have a temple for his home, instead of the pine-tree, and awarded him the title of 'Soldier Pan'.

40. But all that naming and doing was still in the future. On the wedding-night, as soon as it was dark, the revellers one and all escorted the bridal couple to the room where they were to sleep— some were blowing on pan-pipes, and some on flutes, while others were holding aloft big torches. And when they were near the bedroom doors, they started to sing with harsh and strident voices, for all the world as if they were breaking up the ground with three-pronged forks instead of singing the hymn to Hymen!* But Daphnis and Chloe lay down naked together, wrapped their arms about each other, and began to kiss; and the amount of time they spent awake that night would have put even

little owls* in the shade! And Daphnis did a thing or two that Lycaenion had taught him. And now Chloe learned for the first time that all their exploits in the greenwood were just

GAMES THAT SHEPHERDS PLAY.

EXPLANATORY NOTES

3 *Preface*: for an explanation of the line-division which I have employed in this passage and in 1.14 and 18, 2.7 and 34, 3.34, and 4.8, see Introduction, pp. xx–xxii.

5 *About two hundred stades*: nearly 23 miles. There are approximately eight and a half stades to a mile.

Lamon: this name is very rare, and has no clear etymology in Greek.

recognition-tokens: Gk. *gnōrismata*, objects left with an exposed baby as attestations of its identity. Such tokens are a stock device in the recognition-scenes of Greek plays and romances.

Myrtale: 'Myrtle-woman', from Gk. *myrtos*, myrtle. The final *e* in this name is sounded, as also in the feminine names Nape (1.6), Chloe (1.6), Cleariste (4.13), Sophrone (4.21), and Agele (4.39).

6 *Daphnis*: there was a legendary goatherd called Daphnis, whose mother had exposed him under a laurel bush (Gk. *daphnē*), whence his name. See Theocritus, *Idylls* 1.19 and 64 ff. (with Gow's introduction to this Idyll) and 7.72 ff. Longus alludes to the earlier Daphnis elsewhere (see my notes on pp. 15 and 22), and he probably intends the reader to regard this Daphnis as in some fashion prefiguring his own Daphnis. For a discussion of this point, see R. L. Hunter, *A Study of 'Daphnis and Chloe'* (Cambridge, 1983), 22–31.

Dryas: 'Oak-man', from Gk. *drȳs*, oak.

7 *Nape*: 'Glen'. It is the Greek word *napē*, glen, valley.

Chloe: *chloē* is the Greek word for the fresh, new verdure of early spring, which Dryas, as a shepherd, would eagerly await every year. One might translate the name 'Chloe' as 'April grass'.

8 *a cage for a grasshopper or a cricket*: Longus has in mind Theocritus, *Idylls* 1.52, where a little boy makes a cage for a grasshopper or a cricket by plaiting rushes and asphodel-stalks.

reeds: the 'reeds' (*kalamoi*) which were used in the making of pan-pipes are not to be confused with the rushes of English lakes, but were the plant called *Arundo donax* or Giant Reed, 'a tall bamboo-like reed with tough woody leafy stems thicker than a finger . . . the largest grass in Europe' (O. Polunin and A. Huxley, *Flowers of the Mediterranean* (London, 1981), 199). Such reeds are employed as fishing-rods in 2.12, and Syrinx hides in a bed of them (2.34). In translating the *kalamoi* of pan-pipes as 'reeds' throughout, I have followed the English convention; but 'canes' or 'bamboos' would be a more accurate rendering. There is, of course, no question of a *vibrating* reed in connection with pan-pipes.

9 *orgyia*: there are about six feet to an orgyia.

10 *the broad band of cloth*: Gk. *tainia*. This article of female attire has been correctly described by Margaret Anne Doody, *The True Story of the Novel* (London, 1997), 493.

12 *Dorcon*: *dorkōn* is one of the Greek words for 'roe deer'.

13 *nestlings brought from the mountains*: perhaps nestling falcons, to be trained for hawking.

    Satyrs: these mythical attendants on Dionysus had beards.

14 *more colourless than grass at high summer*: Longus here echoes a line of the Lesbian poetess Sappho (7th–6th cent. BC), 'and I am paler than withered grass' (fragment 31.14–15, ed. Lobel and Page), in a description of the symptoms of intense passion.

15 *but Daphnis is withering*: an allusion to how love causes the cowherd Daphnis to waste away in Theocritus, *Idylls* 1.66–141 and 7.71–7.

16 *green elm-bark*: the inner bark of the elm has anti-inflammatory properties. See Edmund Launert, *The Hamlyn Guide to Edible and Medicinal Plants of Britain and Northern Europe* (London, 1989), 120. Also ibid. 10: 'Occasionally, especially in folk medicine, plants are applied directly to the affected part of the body', rather than after infusion, decoction, etc.

17 *the proverbial 'wolf's mouth'*: 'Out of the wolf's mouth' was a Greek proverb applied to those who enjoyed some stroke of luck against all expectation. It was derived from the fable of Aesop in which a heron puts his head between a wolf's jaws to remove a bone. When the heron claims his promised reward, the wolf replies: 'Are you not content to have got your head safely *out of a wolf's mouth*, but must ask for a reward as well?' See *Fables of Aesop*, translated by S. A. Handford (Harmondsworth, 1978), no. 29.

20 *Pyrrha*: a small town situated on the Gulf of Kalloni, a deep indentation in the south-west coast of Lesbos. It was therefore on the opposite side of the island to Mytilene, which faces north-east.

    a Carian hemiolia: there are two points here. (1) The people of Caria in Asia Minor were regarded by the Greeks as foreigners, and they were notorious pirates. Thus when some Greeks of Pyrrha set out to plunder their neighbours, they use a Carian ship to cloak their identity. (2) Their ship, a *hemiolia*, was a type of vessel popular with pirates in the fourth century BC, see Introduction, p. xiv. In fact the identical phrase, 'a Carian *hemiolia*', is used to describe a pirate-ship by an unknown fourth-century orator quoted in the *Etymologicum Magnum* 430.39. The *hemiolia* probably had one-and-a-half files of oars a side (*hemiolios* means 'one-and-a-half'), half of the oars being single-manned and half double-manned. Such ships were fast, and had space in the bow for fighting-men, hence their suitability for piracy. See the description by J. S. Morrison in *The International Journal of Nautical Archaeology and Underwater Exploration*, 9:2 (1980), 121–6.

fragrant wine: see note to p. 70.

as he walked idly near the sea: Longus intends an allusion to the Homeric Hymn to Dionysus, in which the god is captured by Tyrrhenian pirates as he walks beside the sea. He is carried aboard their ship, but terrifies them by assuming the shape of a lion; they jump overboard, and are changed into dolphins.

22 *as if he were driving a wagon*: perhaps a glance at *Odyssey* 5.370 ff., where the ship of Odysseus breaks up in a storm sent by Poseidon. 'But Odysseus got astride one of the planks, like someone mounted on a riding horse, and stripped off his clothes . . . and then he plunged forward into the sea.' The episode of the stolen cows is closely parallel to a story in Aelian's work *On the Characteristics of Animals* 8.19, where swineherds recover their pigs from a pirate ship by shouting their customary cry from the shore. 'When the pigs heard it, they all pushed to one side of the ship and capsized it. And so the evildoers straightaway drowned, and the pigs swam away to their rightful masters.' This story was known to the elder Pliny, who mentions it in his *Natural History* 8.208. See the remarks of O. Schönberger in his commentary on *Daphnis and Chloe* (3rd edition, Berlin 1980), 182.

lamenting for their dead master: just as in Theocritus, *Idylls* 1.71–5 cattle and wild animals lament for Daphnis as he wastes away.

24 *withies*: I have rendered as 'withies' Longus' plural *lugous*, which refers to the long (3 ft. to 9 ft.) branches of the *vitex* shrub, also called *agnus castus* or *chaste-tree*. In Mediterranean countries this shrub grows along rivers, beside mountain torrents, and in damp places beside the sea. Its branches are tough and flexible, and can be used as tethers or twisted into ropes, as in 2.13. When dry, they provide the bars of bird cages or, as here, serve as tapers. In northern Europe, where the *vitex* is not native, willow-wands are used for similar purposes. The word 'withies' (sing. 'withy') properly denotes willow-wands, but is also applied to *vitex* branches, for which no separate word exists in English. The *vitex* shrub is described and illustrated in Polunin and Huxley, *Flowers of the Mediterranean*, 154 and fig. 394. See also Merry and Riddell on *Odyssey* 9.427.

for conveying the grape-juice after dark: lest it deteriorate by being left in the wine-press until the next day.

low-growing: 'It [i.e. the vine] is cut near the root, and allowed to extend its branches laterally.' A. Henderson (1824), describing the viticulture of the Greek islands in his own day. Cited by Charles Seltman, *Wine in the Ancient World* (London, 1957), 74.

Bacchante: in mythology, a female follower of the god Dionysus; in real life, a woman devoted to the worship of this god.

25 *Old Philetas*: some scholars have suggested that this name is intended to evoke the Greek poet Philetas of Cos (*fl. c.*290 BC), who was honoured by the Roman poets of the late Republic and early Empire as their model for

the writing of love-poetry in the elegiac metre. This theory is plausible, insofar that several of these poets (Propertius, Tibullus, Ovid) adopted, in all likelihood from Philetas of Cos, the role of 'instructor in love' (*praeceptor amoris*), which is the character that Longus gives to old Philetas here; while at 2.35 below Philetas emerges as a notable musician. Longus could scarcely have known the poems of Philetas of Cos at first hand, since there is no evidence that they survived after the first century AD. But he might have acquired some knowledge of them from imitations and paraphrases made by Greek poets, and from quotations in commentaries. See the discussion in Hunter, *A Study*, 76–83.

25 *the Nymphs here*: Philetas gestures to the cave.

   Pan yonder: a statue of Pan stood nearby, see 2.23.

27 *far-spreading herd of cattle*: adapted from the Homeric phrase 'far-spreading herds of goats', *Iliad* 2.474; *Odyssey* 14.101, and elsewhere.

   he has such power as even Zeus has not: on Philetas' description of the powers of the cosmogonic Eros, see Introduction, pp. xxiv–xxv.

28 *For there is no remedy for Love . . .*: the last sentence is adapted, with significant variation, from the eleventh Idyll of Theocritus, addressed to the poet's friend Nicias of Miletus, who was a physician and poet: 'I think there is no remedy for love, Nicias, nothing to be smeared or sprinkled on, but only the Muses; soothing and sweet indeed for mortals is this cure, but hard to find' (*Idylls* 11.1–4).

30 *Methymna*: Methymna (today also called Molivos) is a town on the north coast of Lesbos, about 38 miles from Mytilene. In what follows, Longus has turned to account the rivalry between the two places, which existed as early as the seventh century BC.

33 *like a cloud of starlings or jackdaws*: in *Iliad* 17.755–9, the Achaeans fleeing from Aeneas and Hector are compared to starlings and jackdaws fleeing before a hawk. In Longus' simile, however, the smaller birds are the attackers.

36 *whom you and Chloe have never honoured*: in making the Nymph rebuke Daphnis and Chloe for their failure to worship Pan, Longus alludes to an identical reproach, uttered by the god himself on a famous occasion in Greek history. Before the battle of Marathon in 490 BC, the Athenians sent the runner Philippides to Sparta with an appeal for help. On his return to Athens, Philippides asserted that, while crossing Mt Parthenion above Tegea, he had fallen in with Pan, who had addressed him by name and told him to ask the Athenians why they payed him no devotion, although he was their friend and had helped them in the past and would do so again. After their victory, the Athenians made a shrine for Pan in a cavern under the Acropolis, and celebrated in his honour annual sacrifices and a torch-race (Herodotus 6.105). It was said that Pan helped the Athenians again at Salamis in 480 BC, and he was also credited with

defending Delphi against the Galatians, during their invasion under Brennus, 279 BC.

38 *O men . . . deeds?*: Pan's opening words reproduce, with slight variation, the admonition uttered to Aristodicus by the oracle of Apollo at Didyma (on this oracle see below, note to p. 74) when Aristodicus took away the birds which nested in the prophetic shrine: 'O most unholy of men, why do you venture on these brazen deeds? Will you carry off the suppliants from my temple as your plunder?' (Herodotus 1.159.3).

45 *When . . .*: sections 1 and 2, and the first sentence of section 3, are composed in a style calculated to suggest the tone of a historical writer, and the Greek text contains echoes of expressions used by Herodotus, Thucydides, and Xenophon. Longus intends humorous irony, by describing the war between two provincial towns in terms appropriate for the epic struggles of Greece against Persia and Athens against Sparta.

47 *But . . . snow!*: in this sentence, Longus paraphrases a line or two of some lost Greek poet. I have taken the words 'thorough flood, thorough fire' from Shakespeare, *A Midsummer Night's Dream*, II. i. 10.

48 *Now . . .*: the manuscripts differ considerably from one another in this sentence and in the four succeeding sentences, 'There was', etc. I have translated the text of M. D. Reeve (see Note on the Text and Translation, p. xxx n. 1), who for the most part accepts the reconstruction proposed by R. Hercher (1858).

49 *a ram lamb*: lit. 'a year-old ram'.

51 *Itys*: the son of Tereus, king of Thrace, and Procne, a princess of Athens. Tereus raped Procne's sister, Philomela, then cut out her tongue to silence her. She wove the story of her wrong on a piece of tapestry, which she sent to Procne. Procne took vengeance on Tereus by serving him with the flesh of Itys. When Tereus discovered the truth, he tried to murder the two women, but the gods saved them by turning Tereus into a hoopoe, Philomela into a swallow, and Procne into a nightingale, in which shape she ever laments for Itys.

52 *Chromis*: a name of uncertain derivation, occurring several times in epic and pastoral poetry.

53 *Lycaenion*: 'Little she-wolf'. This name is a diminutive form of Gk. *lykaina*, she-wolf.

she told Chromis . . .: the same stratagem appears in Aristophanes, *Ecclesiazusae* (*Women at the Assembly*) 528 ff.

my twenty geese: the twenty geese and the eagle come from *Odyssey* 19.535 ff., where Penelope dreams that her twenty (real) geese have been killed by an eagle, the geese standing for her suitors and the eagle for Odysseus.

56 *boatswain*: in a trireme, according to Xenophon, the boatswain was responsible for keeping the rowers in good heart, and it depended on him

whether they performed well or badly (*Oeconomicus* 21.3, quoted by J. S. Morrison and J. F. Coates, *The Athenian Trireme* (Cambridge, 1986), 112). In the case of Longus' fishing-boat, however, the crew are not numerous enough to allow for a designated boatswain, but take turns at the job. Hence the change to a plural, 'the boatswains', later in this section, and in section 22.

59 *We're poor folk ... a rich bridegroom*: some textual corruption has deprived Myrtale's opening sentences of logical coherence.

61 *tribola*: the *tribola* was a heavy wooden board, studded on its underside with flints or iron teeth, which was dragged over the harvested corn in order to detach the grain from the chaff. Similar implements are still used in parts of the Mediterranean region and the Middle East. See K. D. White, *Agricultural Implements of the Roman World* (Cambridge, 1967), 155.

63 *yet one apple ...*: in his description of the solitary apple, Longus has adapted some phrases from a poem of Sappho which we possess only in a three-line fragment: 'like as the fair sweet-apple blushes on the topmost twig, | high on the topmost twig, and the apple-pickers have forgotten it— | but no! 'twas not forgotten; they could not win up to it, rather' (fragment 105(a), ed. Lobel and Page). In Sappho's lines, which are from an *epithalamium* or marriage-song, the apple is a symbol for the bride, who has been kept safe for her husband. When Daphnis picks the apple for Chloe, therefore, the situation contains an element of symbolism derived from literary allusion, as well as exemplifying the immemorial Greek belief that the giving and receiving of an apple implies the offering and acceptance of love. This passage also owes something to the description of Nature's prodigality in Theocritus, *Idylls* 7.131 ff., esp. 143–5: 'Everything smelt of summer full rich and of the fruit-harvest. Pears in plenty rolled at our feet, and apples by our side.'

64 *a prize for beauty*: Daphnis alludes to the golden apple which Paris presented to Aphrodite, in preference to Hera and Athena, at their contest of beauty on Mt Ida.

65 *pleasure-ground*: the word used by Longus, *paradeisos*, comes from Persian and properly denotes a walled park containing wild beasts, where the Persian king and nobles hunted. There is no big game in Longus' paradise, which is a garden and arboretum, but the royal associations of the word are acknowledged, see 4.2.

four plethra: there are 100 feet to one plethron.

All kinds of trees grew there ...: behind this elaborate description stands the celebrated description of King Alcinous' garden in *Odyssey* 7.112 ff., where there were 'pear-trees and pomegranate-trees and apple-trees with bright fruit, and sweet fig-trees and luxuriant olives', as well as a vineyard with grapes just turning purple, beds of herbs, and (as in section 4 below) water.

66 *Semele giving him birth* ...: the infant Dionysus was plucked from Semele's ashes after she had been incinerated by Zeus' lightnings; Dionysus found Ariadne as she lay asleep on the island of Naxos, where Theseus had abandoned her on his homeward voyage after killing the Minotaur; Lycurgus, while chasing the nurses of Dionysus, was checked and bound fast by vine-tendrils; Pentheus, the king of Thebes, tried to imprison Dionysus, but was torn apart by the Maenads on Mt Cithaeron. Dionysus' conquest of the Indians was a favourite theme in Greek poetry of the Roman Empire. For Dionysus and the Tyrrhenian pirates, see note to p. 20.

67 *Eudromus*: 'Good runner'.

69 *just like Apollo did to Marsyas*: Marsyas, a satyr, presumed to challenge Apollo to a contest of piping. The god won, flayed Marsyas alive, and hung his skin from a tree.

70 *Astylus*: 'Townee', from Gk. *asty*, town. The name is mildly derogatory, and expresses Longus' preference for the country over the city.

parasite: Gk. *parasitos*, 'table-companion', someone provided with meals by a rich man in return for stimulating conversation. Such 'parasites' might be anything from austere philosophers to drunken buffoons.

Gnathon: the *o* is long. This name means, approximately, 'Jaws', from Gk. *gnathos*, jaw.

fragrant wine: Gk. *anthosmias*, a red wine which was prized for its flowery bouquet. At Eresos in Lesbos, according to Athenaeus, it was made by adding one part of sea-water to fifty parts of grape-juice (*Deipnosophistae* 1.32b, ed. Kaibel).

71 *Dionysophanes and his wife Cleariste*: the name Dionysophanes means 'Dionysus appearing'. See Introduction, p. xxvi. Cleariste's name ('Best fame') indicates high social status.

72 *If Apollo ever herded cattle*: Poseidon and Apollo agreed to serve King Laomedon of Troy for a year, Poseidon building the city-walls and Apollo herding Laomedon's cattle. When the king refused to pay them, Poseidon sent a sea-monster, Apollo a plague (*Iliad* 21.441 ff.).

74 *Apollo kissed him*: in a grove at Didyma in Caria, Asia Minor. Apollo gave Branchus the gift of prophecy.

the Lord of All: there is an alternative manuscript reading: 'Zeus' instead of 'the Lord of All'.

76 *Sophrone*: the baby's nurse. The name means 'Chastity' or 'Chaste woman'. There is a nurse of this name in Menander, *Epitrepontes* (*The Arbitrants*) 1062.

79 *Lampis the cowherd*: the despoiler of Lamon's flowers, see 4.7.

83 *the customary offering to Hermes*: Hermes receives the final offering because he brings sleep.

83 *who occupied the last place*: that is, Megacles was reclining furthest to the right, in a place of honour next to his host, and was consequently the last to be shown the tokens. So in Plato, *Symposium* 175c Socrates shares the last couch with Agathon, the host.

financing choruses and fitting out triremes: Longus alludes to the tax-obligations imposed on the wealthiest citizens at Athens in the fifth and fourth centuries BC. A *chorēgus* ('chorus-leader') had to pay the expenses of one of the groups of actors competing at a tragic or comic festival. A *triērarchus* ('trireme-captain') was expected to provide the equipment and crew for a warship, and to make up any deficiencies in the pay and rations provided by the state; he might also command the vessel on active service. See Morrison and Coates, *The Athenian Trireme*, 108 ff. So Megacles had been very rich indeed—as his name ('Greatly famous') implies. This passage shows that Longus intended the dramatic date of his story to be the fifth or the fourth century BC.

84 *you'll never credit this*: these words are not in the Greek, but I have put them in to express the amazement and disbelief conveyed by the alliteration of initial *p* in the Greek words *patera poiēsei poimnion*, 'a sheep will make me a father'. Cf. the common Greek exclamation *papai*, 'You don't say!'

'This is . . . Love': Dionysophanes uses elevated language in recognition of the fact that Chloe's salvation has been god-ordained.

Rhoda: 'Rose', from Gk. *rhodon*, rose.

85 *Philopoemen*: 'Friend to shepherds' (Gk. *poimēn*, shepherd).

Agele: 'Herd' (Gk. *agelē*, herd. The *g* is hard).

And . . . old: some editors omit this sentence, which reads somewhat unconvincingly in the Greek.

pictures: despite the plural, it seems natural to take this as a reference to the painting mentioned in the Preface. But the Greek word, *eikonas*, could equally well denote statues or reliefs.

Hymen: the divine patron of weddings.

86 *little owls*: Gk. *glaukes*, that is, owls of the species *Athene noctua*.

An Anthology of Elizabethan Prose Fiction

An Anthology of Seventeenth-Century
    Fiction

Early Modern Women's Writing

Three Early Modern Utopias (Utopia; New
    Atlantis; The Isle of Pines)

FRANCIS BACON   **Essays**
    The Major Works

APHRA BEHN   **Oroonoko and Other Writings**
    The Rover and Other Plays

JOHN BUNYAN   **Grace Abounding**
    The Pilgrim's Progress

JOHN DONNE   **The Major Works**
    Selected Poetry

BEN JONSON   **The Alchemist and Other Plays**
    The Devil is an Ass and Other Plays
    Five Plays

JOHN MILTON   **The Major Works**
    Paradise Lost
    Selected Poetry

SIR PHILIP SIDNEY   **The Old Arcadia**
    The Major Works

IZAAK WALTON   **The Compleat Angler**

American Literature

Authors in Context

British and Irish Literature

Children's Literature

Classics and Ancient Literature

Colonial Literature

Eastern Literature

European Literature

History

Medieval Literature

Oxford English Drama

Poetry

Philosophy

Politics

Religion

The Oxford Shakespeare

A complete list of Oxford World's Classics, including Authors in Context, Oxford English Drama, and the Oxford Shakespeare, is available in the UK from the Marketing Services Department, Oxford University Press, Great Clarendon Street, Oxford OX2 6DP, or visit the website at www.oup.com/uk/worldsclassics.

In the USA, visit www.oup.com/us/owc for a complete title list.

Oxford World's Classics are available from all good bookshops. In case of difficulty, customers in the UK should contact Oxford University Press Bookshop, 116 High Street, Oxford OX1 4BR.

The Oxford World's Classics Website

www.oup.com/uk/worldsclassics

- Information about new titles
- Explore the full range of Oxford World's Classics
- Links to other literary sites and the main OUP webpage
- Imaginative competitions, with bookish prizes
- Articles by editors
- Extracts from Introductions
- Special information for teachers and lecturers

www.oup.com/uk/worldsclassics